BOOKS BY HELENA NEWBURY

Helena Newbury is the *New York Times* and *USA Today* bestselling author of sixteen romantic suspenses, all available where you bought this book. Find out more at helenanewbury.com.

Lying and Kissing

Punching and Kissing

Texas Kissing

Kissing My Killer

Bad For Me

Saving Liberty

Kissing the Enemy

Outlaw's Promise

Alaska Wild

Brothers

Captain Rourke

Royal Guard

Mount Mercy

The Double

Hold Me in the Dark

Deep Woods

PUNCHING AND KISSING

HELENA NEWBURY

FOSTER & BLACK

Cover by Mayhem Cover Creations. Main cover model image licensed from (and copyright remains with) Mr Big Photography/iStockPhoto

ISBN: 978-1-914526-18-3

ACKNOWLEDGMENTS

Thank you to:

My fantastic street team!

Liz, my editor

DB, Pearl, Jenny and Olivia, my beta readers

And to all my readers :)

1

SYLVIE

I didn't belong there.

The crowd was a baying, howling mass of wild eyes and open mouths, leaning far over the concrete balcony to gawp. The heat of a hundred frenzied bodies pressed in on me from all sides until I could barely catch my breath.

I had to get out of there but I needed to stay. I owed it to Alec.

I stumbled through the crowd, making my way around the edge of the huge, circular room. I kept my gaze fixed on the graffiti, on the rusted pipes...anything to avoid looking at what was going on below us.

There was a cry of pain and I glanced down before I could stop myself. One man had the other on the floor, fists pummeling his face. There was only one rule: it went on until someone couldn't get up.

Welcome to The Pit.

I looked away, disgusted, and tried to move faster. Elbowing or pushing isn't in my nature and I was the lone woman in a roomful of hyped-up, drunk men. So I muttered apologies and sneaked through gaps. Luckily, they barely noticed me—not the rich guys who'd come there for an edgy walk on the wild side, not the local guys who were one bad bet away from disaster. Everyone was going nuts, jumping and yelling and punching the air.

No, wait. Not everyone.

I stopped in my tracks as I saw him. He stood like a rock in an ocean, a full head taller than the people around him and moving not even an inch as they ebbed and swelled against him. His broad back was like a cliff and his shoulders seemed twice as wide as mine. He was in a sleeveless top, arms folded across his chest, and the heavy swells of his shoulders and biceps led down to thickly corded forearms. *Big,* and ripped, as well. But it wasn't his size or his muscles that made me stop, nor even the way he stood so still.

His hood was raised, throwing his face into shadow. Who wore a hood, in this heat?

I moved forward and lost sight of him for a moment. When I saw him again, I was closer. I was looking up into that shadowed face, now. I could just catch glimpses: a jaw dusted with dark stubble, a full lower lip pressed into a tight line. He was watching, but he hadn't lost himself like the others. Maybe he was sickened by what was happening downstairs. Maybe, like me, he didn't belong in this place.

I passed behind him, willing myself not to look. I made it three feet beyond him before the urge got too much and I glanced back over my shoulder. At first, I could see only shadows under the hood but then—

As one of the cheap fluorescent tubes flickered, I caught a glimpse of eyes: savagely blue and brutally hard. Starkly beautiful, they saw every weakness and gave no mercy.

I tore my eyes away, panting like I'd just missed a speeding truck. I'd been wrong. He wasn't immune to this place at all—he was already lost. And if I didn't belong here; he could have been born here.

I tried to move faster through the crowd. A drink. I needed a drink. I headed for the guy I'd seen on the far side of the room, the one who sold sodas out of a cooler at six dollars a time. He knew his market—six dollars was nothing to the guys who came here, the ones who bet thousands of dollars and then drove home in their Lexuses, speed-dialing their wives to apologize for working late. To me, six dollars was a day's food. But I was going to pass out if I didn't drink something.

I bought a Dr. Pepper and ran the cool metal can over my forehead, closing my eyes, letting the chill soak into me and calm me, pushing away the remembered fear from when I'd glimpsed that guy's expression.

Fear and...something else.

The eyes had been gorgeous—coldly beautiful beyond anything I'd ever seen. And that jaw, those lips, that body—the expression had sent ice down my spine but, when it reached my groin, it had turned into something else entirely. Cold had become hot. Fear had become—

I closed my eyes for a second and took a deep breath. *Stupid.* Sure, from the glimpses I'd seen, the guy might just be hot as hell under that hood. But that expression...he was like the distilled essence of this place.

Stay. The fuck. Away.

I popped the top and drank. The cold soda foamed down my throat like liquid sex. A calming chill soaked through me and I felt my heart gradually slowing down.

I drained the whole can before I looked up and saw him. The hooded man. Closer, this time, no more than ten feet away.

And staring right at me.

The momentary cool from the soda boiled away in an instant. A wave of heat shot through me, rippling upward from my groin. I wasn't ready for how deeply sexual his gaze was, how it connected with me right where I lived.

I told myself, *of course he's not looking at you.* I'm not much to look at. My brother's the eye-catching one, all blond hair and muscle, like my dad. I take after my mom—small and slender, with boobs like half-oranges.

I wrenched my eyes from him and stared fixedly into the distance, waiting for him to look away.

But I could still feel his gaze on the side of my face, never wavering for a second.

2

AEDAN

There were about a million reasons I shouldn't be there: it was too damn hot; I had to be up early for work the next morning; I didn't want to give *him* the satisfaction of seeing me at one of his fights.

But there was something that mattered more than any of that. That itch, that deep-down itch that can't be scratched any other way but feeling your fists connect. The rush you get as you duck and weave, hands up, taking the punishment and then returning it tenfold.

I don't do that anymore. But the itch is still there. Watching it is the next best thing.

By rights, indulging myself like that should have brought something bad down on me. A lightning bolt from above, maybe. But someone saw fit to send me a whole different kind of divine intervention.

She was the only woman in the place, but she would have stood out if she'd been in some uptown club filled with supermodels. Long, black hair, maybe even darker than mine, so dark it was almost blue-black. A slender, lithe body that made me want to take the flat of my hand and run it all the way down from her neck to the curve of her calf, like stroking a cat. She was wearing a bubblegum-pink *Curious Weasels* t-shirt and it molded to the soft swells of her breasts in a way that made my breath catch.

No. Not her. I wasn't going to torture myself with a girl like that. Too beautiful. Too pure. I didn't deserve someone like that. Oh, sure, I could grab her wrist and pin her with my Irish eyes and tell her she was coming home with me, *now.* Maybe she'd see what was underneath the hood and freak out, but maybe she'd be okay with it. Then we could go back to my apartment. My body between those sweet thighs, driving up into her, those cute little tits filling my hands—

Jesus, would that really be so bad?

Yeah, it would. In the morning, she'd realize I wasn't some fantasy bad boy; I was just *bad.* Not an exciting walk on the wild side but a full-on savage, only good for two things. She'd look down at my big, calloused hands as they roved over her naked breasts and start to think about what else they'd done—how much pain and damage I'd dealt. She'd panic and make excuses and run back to her safe little life, wherever the hell that was, and it'd be over. Or, worse, she'd hang around just long enough for me to fuck up her life. I wasn't going to risk that. No matter how perfect her tits were.

I watched her moving through the crowd. Damn, she was just a scared little thing. Why didn't people make way for her? I pegged her for about twenty, five years younger than me. It was only when she glanced my way again that I saw the pain in her eyes. She *was* about twenty, but she'd seen more bad shit than someone her age should.

She bought a soda and ran the can over her forehead—right there, in front of me, like it was nothing at all. I drank in every detail: the slow roll of the can as it kissed her skin, the soft, long lashes as she closed her eyes in pleasure, the drop of ice water that fell from the bottom of the can and fell—

Jesus onto her upper boob and then trickling down into the scoop neck of her t-shirt, painting a trail of moisture over the soft flesh.

I could feel my cock swell against my thigh. *Damn, she was hot.*

She opened her eyes and I finally got a look at them. Big and liquid and the color of some lush, enchanted forest grove. And her lips! Soft, perfect pillows, flawless and pink. She popped the top of the can and drank. I couldn't take my eyes off that elegant throat, flexing and swallowing. God, she was beautiful. What the hell was she doing here? Some rich kid, slumming it? Her clothes didn't look expensive, but she must be some rich guy's girlfriend. What else would a woman be doing here? This was a guy's world—women had more sense.

And then she looked up and, for maybe half a second, she was looking right at me. A jolt went through my body, as if I'd touched a live wire. I felt every muscle go tense, my hands making fists so tight my knuckles ached. It was like I'd dropped right into a fantasy world for an instant, a heaven where I knew her, where we could be together. I felt like I was coming alive, the last few years beginning to slough off and fall away from me.

An angel. Fate had sent me an angel.

Then she came to her senses and looked away and I felt like an idiot for staring at her. I was pretty sure she couldn't see much, under the hood, but maybe she'd seen. Or maybe she'd sensed what I was like and that had scared her even more.

I couldn't tear my eyes from her, though. I drank her in because it might be the last time I ever saw her. I watched until she finally finished her soda and headed out of the main room, down the long, dark hallway that led to the bathroom. I caught my breath. The sight of her ass in those jeans, pert and tight and just the right size for my hands...I had a new favorite part of her.

She disappeared into the shadows and the spell was broken. Reality returned like a punch to the side of my head. *Yeah, and you'll never even touch her, you feckin' idiot.*

I liked her and that was why I had to stay away from her. Because if I got tempted and actually got close, all I was going to do was hurt her.

And then I frowned, because I saw another guy watching her retreating back. Not one of the rich guys in a suit, one of the locals. He nodded to his two buddies and all three of them disappeared into the shadows.

Oh God, no.

3

SYLVIE

The Pit was some kind of industrial building, once. Most of it is just bare concrete and graffiti, but some of the fluorescent lights still work and there's running water. The crowd has to be able to see; the organizers have to hose the blood off the floor.

Hidden away down a long hallway, in what I guess used to be the office area, there's a bathroom. Not many people know about it. I normally avoid it because I don't like being off on my own in The Pit. But after draining a whole Dr. Pepper, I suddenly needed to go.

The roar of the crowd died away as I turned one corner, then another, hurrying past disused rooms with broken windows. It wasn't much cooler than the rest of The Pit, but at least there was space to think.

Had that guy really been staring at me? It didn't seem likely—no one ever looked at me. I couldn't help thinking someone could have rolled the genetic dice better. I could have been some tall, leggy blonde with bags of confidence and my brother could have been short, dark and shy.

Because then maybe he wouldn't be downstairs, waiting to take his turn in the ring.

I locked myself in the bathroom. There was only one in the whole place, so it's a good thing people don't know it's there or it'd get pretty nasty in there on fight night. I pushed my jeans and panties down around my knees. A few seconds later...*relief.*

I understood why Alec was doing it. Without the cash from fighting, we'd be on the street already. But watching him risk his life each month was almost unbearable. I hated The Pit. But sitting waiting for him at home...that would be even worse.

I was just about to stand up when the door rattled. Not hard, just like someone was leaning against it, but it made me jump. I cleared my throat. *"Occupied!"* I called out, wishing my voice didn't sound so high and nervy.

A low laugh, the sort that's shared between friends. And then I saw the bolt on the door slide back.

I grabbed for it, but it was too late. The door was swinging wide and the guy was already inside. Not much taller than me but wider, with heavy muscle under a layer of fat. He was still holding the coin he'd used to open the lock from the outside.

I started to get up. I wasn't all that scared, yet. My mind was still occupied with humiliation, one hand reaching for my jeans while the other tried to cover my groin. In my head, it was more on the level of some high school prank where the guys invade the girls' bathroom and laugh at them.

Then his hand slapped across my mouth, his sweaty palm tight against my lips. With his other hand, he lifted me off the toilet and pressed me against the wall. Two more men were crowding in, almost filling the small room. And the true horror of it began to sink in.

One guy closed and locked the door. I could barely hear the roar of the distant crowd, now—even if I could scream, no one would hear me. *And no one knows I'm in here.*

The guy holding me had wiry brown hair that lay in tangled curls. His foot, when he stamped it down on my jeans and panties to ram them down my legs, was in a work boot, white with dust. I felt my legs bared, then his knee between them, stopping them from closing.

I tried to scream, but my lungs couldn't get any air. In his excitement, the guy had pushed the edge of his hand right up against my nostrils. I tried to kick, but my ankles were still tangled in my jeans and the bundle of cloth was pinned to the floor by his foot. I heaved myself away from the wall, but his chest was pressed hard against me.

I still couldn't breathe. Every panicked attempt just sucked his hand tighter against my nose and mouth.

His other hand pushed between my legs. Fingers on me. God...*in* me. I wanted to throw up. I clawed with my hands and managed to scratch his neck, but then one of the other men grabbed my wrists and pressed my hands hard against the wall. All three of them were laughing, the sound ringing in my ears. I heard a belt buckle being unfastened.

I was still straining against their grip, but my vision was going dark. I wondered if I was going to pass out before it happened.

The door gave a single, solitary creak, as if someone was leaning against it. I looked towards it—anything was better than looking at the men's faces.

With a sound like the end of the world, the door was ripped off its hinges and lifted away, trailing shattered wood. Then it was tossed aside and I saw—

Him. The man who'd been staring at me.

The lead guy's two buddies ran at my savior, yelling at him. Now my arms were free, but I barely had the strength to lift them away from the wall. My body had gone limp, my lungs burning for air.

The hooded guy grabbed the first man by the t-shirt and hurled him across the hallway as easily as if he was tossing a garbage bag into a dumpster. The man hit the wall with a sickening crack and went down.

The other man tried to land a punch. Mystery guy blocked it easily, then slammed his fist into the man's side, right over his kidney. The man crumpled, just in time to get a knee to his chin.

My vision had narrowed to a tunnel. My face was wet with sweat, my life measured in seconds, now. The guy holding me glanced between me and my rescuer like a predator unwilling to let go of its meal. He finally released me and turned to run.

The hooded guy took a single step forward and slammed a fist up into the man's chin. The uppercut lifted him off his feet and his head smacked into the top of the door frame. He crashed unconscious to the floor.

I slid to the floor. I was wavering at the edge of consciousness, barely capable of taking a breath, but my tortured lungs managed one weak little gasp. The fetid air of The Pit poured down my throat and it tasted like it came from the Swiss Alps. I took another breath and another, each one a little stronger, until I was gulping it down. It took long seconds for my vision to clear and, when it did, nausea followed it. I wrapped my arms around myself and just sat there, staring at the floor.

My rescuer's boots stepped into my vision. Then his knees appeared as he crouched down. I didn't look up at him—I couldn't. I felt as if I was going to throw up. My jeans and panties were still around my ankles but I couldn't pull them up while I was sitting and it didn't feel like my legs would hold me if I tried to stand. I settled for pressing my knees together and hugging my calves tight to my thighs. I hoped most of me was hidden in shadow.

I could feel him watching me. Waiting. Giving me time.

I was shaking. I couldn't stop shaking.

He didn't say anything and he didn't attempt to touch me. I think I would have screamed, if he had. He just crouched there next to me, guarding me. I don't know how long I sat there—minutes, at least. Once, I heard someone approach down the corridor and saw his head snap up. "*Fuck off,*" he snapped, and the person scurried away.

Except it didn't sound like *Fuck off.* It sounded more like *Feck off.* He had an unfamiliar accent that reminded me of cold, unyielding rock.

At last, I felt strong enough to try to stand. I pushed myself unsteadily to my feet, trying to pull my jeans up at the same time, knowing that whatever I did, he was going to catch a glimpse of my pussy.

But instead, as he stood up with me, I saw him twist and look off down the hallway. He kept his eyes averted while I got my jeans pulled up and only looked back when all the rustling of clothes had ceased.

Now that I was standing, I could see more of him—all the way up to his chest. But I still didn't dare look up at his face. I was burning up inside with humiliation and raw, sick fear. I knew, on some level, that it was over and that I was safe, now. But I'd been shaken on a deeper level. I'd thought I'd known how shitty the world was, how terrifyingly, casually evil men could be, but I'd been wrong.

I was safe, but I'd never feel safe again.

And then he did something—he put his hand out towards me. A big, calloused hand, each finger easily twice the thickness of mine. He didn't touch me with it. He just rested it in the air, an inch away from cupping my shoulder. He left it there, saying nothing.

And I felt a warmth flow through me, expanding outward from that almost-touch. Reassurance that he wasn't like them. That he'd never, ever hurt me.

It shouldn't have been possible from someone who'd just dealt such violence. But I knew it was true.

I finally looked up at him. His hood was still up, his face hidden in shadow. His comforting hand was still almost touching my shoulder, but it wasn't enough. I needed to see *him,* not a mystery savior.

I stared up into the shadows, my eyes pleading.

Slowly, reluctantly, he pulled back his hood just enough to show his face.

Soft black hair cut short and messed up. His strong brow was creasing into a frown at having to reveal himself. But he didn't look angry—not with me, at least. His gorgeous, electric blue eyes seemed to burn with concern. It was when he glanced down at the three men on the floor that I saw the look change to hatred.

The dark stubble on his cheeks made his skin look even paler. Black hair, white skin, blue eyes and that strong brow...I knew that look, but I was way too messed up, right then, to place it.

I saw the fight again in my head. It had been so *quick!* I'd seen plenty of fights in The Pit, but nothing like that. He'd hit with unstoppable power. It had been like watching the men get hit by a truck.

I was still shaking, but it seemed to be dying down. I wrapped my arms around myself and that felt better. But his presence felt better still. It made no sense. I'd seen him destroy those three guys—I should have been terrified of him. But I felt...protected.

"Are you okay?" he asked. That granite-hard accent again, brutal yet beautiful.

He kept glancing down at the guy on the floor—the leader, the one who'd had me pinned against the wall. He was giving the guy such a look of pure, undiluted *hate* that I thought the floor was going to start bubbling and melting. The guy was still breathing—for now. But I realized with a lurch that whether he lived or died depended on my answer.

It scared the hell out of me...but it was strangely reassuring, too. I nodded.

"You're crying," he said tightly. The accent went with his looks, somehow, but my overloaded brain refused to process it. This time his gaze swept around all three of the fallen men, as if he was considering snapping each of them over his knee in turn. *Ending* them, so they could never hurt anyone again.

"I'm okay," I said. I pawed at my cheeks. I *was* crying. Big, fat tears of despair or relief—I didn't know when they'd started, but they seemed to be stopping.

He stared down at me, his eyes full of sadness. And he moved his hand back from my shoulder and offered it to me.

I slowly took it, my small hand almost disappearing as he clasped it in his much bigger one. He drew me away from the bathroom, leading me down the corridor with a gentleness completely at odds with his strength. With every step we took, I breathed a little more easily. I knew that what had happened was going to live on in my nightmares for a long time—maybe forever—but I felt the strength returning to my body.

As we moved through the dimly-lit corridor, I started to glance up at him. The sheer size of him, up close, was imposing. It wasn't just that he was big; it was the hardness of him, as if he was carved from rock under his jeans and hooded top. He didn't seem to have an ounce of fat on him but he probably weighed close to twice what I did. And I swore he wasn't even breathing hard, as if beating those guys up had been nothing at all.

"Thank you," I said, because I realized I hadn't said it yet.

He shrugged awkwardly, glancing back at the three men on the floor.

I was slowly taking in how gorgeous he was. The strong jaw and heavy brow, softened just enough by high cheekbones...and those eyes, pale blue and alive with a fierce, protective fire. I flushed at the memory of how I'd lusted after him when I'd seen him in the crowd. It was fate's cruel trick—the man who'd seen me at my worst was the one I would have liked to see me at my best. As I blinked back the last of the tears, I pleaded silently, *don't remember me like this.*

He stared at me...and then he nodded. As if he could read my mind, as if we'd known each other for years. His grip was warm and comforting and, looking at where we joined, it felt...*right,* somehow. I didn't feel as if I was in danger, despite everything I'd seen him do.

"What's your name?" I asked. "I'm Sylvie."

"Aedan," he said reluctantly. And the name finally helped my brain make the connection between his looks and that flint-like accent. *Irish.* "You going back in there?" he asked, jerking his head down the hall towards the fight. "It's not safe."

"I have to. My brother's in the next fight," I blurted.

He stared at me, probably confused by the lack of family resemblance. "The blond fella? *Koning?*"

I nodded, surprised that he actually knew our surname. Real names weren't used much. The fight organizers gave people stage names to hype them up. Alec was *The Dutchman.* For Aedan to know his surname, he must be pretty close to the scene, more than just another spectator—

Of course. He was a fighter, or maybe an ex-fighter. I didn't recognize him, but then I'd only been going to the fights since Alec got involved.

Aedan shook his head, looking even more troubled, now. The shake dislodged the hood and it fell the rest of the way, exposing his neck. He'd been....*ruined* there. It wasn't just a simple, raised scar. I could see where something had cut deep and then twisted, tearing as it went. Then the wounds had been inexpertly stitched up and thick scars had formed, stretching down under his collar.

I felt my heart tear in two. It wasn't that it was ugly. It was that someone had done something so vicious and cruel to him. I wanted to tell him that it was okay, that it didn't make him any less beautiful. But like an idiot, I just stood there, staring.

He caught me looking and jerked his hood back up, throwing his face into shadow. I cursed myself, trying to think of a way to apologize, but the damage was done.

"I gotta go," he said, and dropped my hand.

I felt something wrench, soul-deep. This was wrong. I knew, somehow, that he was important—maybe the most important person who'd ever walked into my life. But he was already walking, his powerful shoulders squared as if to fend off any attempt to stop him. With his hood up and his back turned, he was suddenly closed off and distant.

And alone.

"Wait!" My hand was tingling where he'd held it. I grabbed it in my other hand, not wanting to lose that warm glow. "How do I find you again?"

He kept walking. I could hear the sudden bitterness in his voice. "You don't."

4

AEDAN

Feck. What the hell had I been thinking? Sure, I'd had to go pull those bastards off her, but I shouldn't have started talking to her. If I really wanted the best for her, I had to stay the hell away from her.

Even now, I could feel my hands unconsciously forming fists, my knuckles cracking as I thought about what they'd done. What they would've done, if I hadn't followed her down that hallway.

Her *brother*. Koning was her brother. Shit.

I'd come to watch the fight because I needed to scratch that itch. Once, I'd been happy with that bloodlust inside me. I'd accepted it as part of me. But then I'd been woken up, in the ugliest way possible, to what I was. A thug. A beast. The more I fought, the worse I got. So I'd stopped, and now I hung around on the fringes of society instead. A non-life: working to keep me busy, fucking, a little drinking to take the edge off. Just whiling away the hours. I stayed away from my old life.

And yet I still came to the fights.

I realized I was rubbing at the scars on my neck, and pulled my hand away.

There was a fight at The Pit most weeks, but I only came once a month or so. Probably why I hadn't run into her before. Sylvie. My angel had a name, now. And fate was laughing at me. *Her brother!* I had to get out of there, *now.* I'd come to watch the fight, but suddenly I couldn't stand to see it. Suddenly, it wasn't just two guys in the ring. Suddenly, it was personal.

I headed for the door. I had to fight the urge to look over my shoulder and try to catch another glimpse of her.

Alec Koning was her brother. I'd been around the scene enough that I could peg a fighter's chances just by looking at him. I'd seen Alec when he'd arrived and I knew his opponent, a guy called Morgan. *"Ripper"* Morgan.

Sylvie's brother was going to get annihilated.

5

SYLVIE

The tiny, pipe-lined rooms where the fighters got ready were meant to be off-limits to the audience. But after what happened, I needed Alec.

Going downstairs meant negotiating a rusting metal stairwell, sticky with spider webs and barely lit. Being somewhere dark, on my own, was the last thing I wanted right now. But the guys Aedan had fought weren't getting up any time soon.

The thought of Aedan made my heart skip in a way it hadn't in a long time. Thoughts of boyfriends had been off my radar for so long that I'd almost forgotten what that felt like—that lift you get inside, when you think of his face, the little shiver that goes down your spine when you hear his voice.

Crazy. Okay, sure, he'd helped me, but he'd ripped through those guys as if they were made of paper. He was obviously some kind of fighter, embedded deep into this world that Alec and I only fleetingly touched once a week. Not a guy anyone would want to get involved with. And yet....

And yet I couldn't stop thinking about him. The pain I'd seen in those pale blue eyes, the way he'd seemed so...*protective* of me. Before I'd driven him away by staring at his scars. *Idiot!*

It was all irrelevant, anyway. I didn't have room in my life for a boyfriend. Every day since Dad died had been about getting by, scraping together the money from my hotel maid's job and Alec's construction work and figuring which bills we could get away without paying. It had been getting harder, since both of us had our shifts cut.

The only thing that had kept us going was Alec's fighting. Rick, the guy who organized the fights, paid him a flat fee with a bonus if he won. The big money, of course, was in the gambling. The rich thought nothing of putting thousands on a fighter to win, or to draw first blood. But we never saw any of that. We didn't have the money to put any bets on ourselves, even if we'd dared to risk it.

Tonight, Alec had to win. He'd won every time so far, thank God, and hadn't gotten too badly hurt. Tonight's win would give us enough money that maybe it could be the last one. It would buy us some breathing room, at least. I could job hunt and maybe find something better paid than the maid job. Alec could do some of those community college courses and move up a little at the construction site—learn wiring or plumbing or something.

If he won.

I emerged into the cramped little room where Alec sat. With his olive-green tank top and cut-off jeans, he could have been some guy chilling on a beach. That's what he should have been doing, instead of risking his life to pay our bills. Great cheekbones, blond hair—my brother had it all going on. He should have been a lifeguard or a DJ or something, knee-deep in adoring women. Not sitting there in this overheated tomb, maybe minutes away from—

My mind rebelled against it. *Please let him be okay, tonight,* I offered up to whoever was listening.

Alec turned and his face lit up as he saw me. "Hey!" Then he frowned and jumped to his feet. He must have been able to see I'd been crying. "What happened?"

I shook my head. "Nothing. Some guys shook me up."

His face hardened into a snarl. "Who? Where?" He glanced upstairs, ready to run up there.

I pulled him into a hug. "It's all over," I told him. "They're dealt with." I squeezed him close. "Somebody came along and beat the crap out of them."

"Who?" His voice was surly, now. I knew what it was—he felt guilty he hadn't been there, and now he needed to know every detail.

I squeezed him harder. "It's okay. Just some Irish guy. I think he fights here, or he used to."

Very slowly, he stepped back so that he could see me properly. "*Irish?*"

I nodded, confused by how shaken he looked.

"Not *Aedan O'Harra?* The one with the scars?"

Now *I* stepped back. "Yeah."

His eyes had gone wild. "Sylvie, *stay away* from that guy."

"Because he used to fight here? *You* fight here!"

He shook his head. "He didn't just fight here. He fucking demolished anyone who set foot in the pit. He's the meanest son of a bitch anyone's ever seen. A *legend.*" He lowered his voice and took my hands. "Sylvie, he's a real bastard. I heard—"

At that moment, someone else descended the stairs. I recognized the footsteps all too well: unhurried steps in expensive leather shoes and an accompanying clang and rattle of metal. My mind had been spinning with what Alec had told me, but suddenly raw fear pushed all that aside. I felt my shoulders tense up. Alec squeezed my hands. But I could see that he was just as scared as me.

"*Well,*" said a voice from the doorway. "Isn't this cute?"

Rick scared the crap out of me. Rick scared the crap out of everyone.

Once, about twenty years ago, Rick had probably been an okay kid. Then—the story goes—his dad beat him so bad his leg didn't heal right. Little Rick got a walking stick. And maybe from the pain in his leg, maybe from his dad's cruelty, he developed a mean streak. The sort of kid who beat stray dogs with a car aerial until, exhausted and terrified, they'd fight one another.

Twenty years on, he'd moved up to people.

He got through most days, from what I'd seen, by downing coffee and snorting coke. It had left him thin, his eyes bulging from his skull. Not a guy who'd win in a fight. So he'd traded his wooden walking stick for an aluminum cane, vicious as a baseball bat but less conspicuous on the street. It was a gaudy thing with a crystal on top as big as my fist. He kept it polished and he didn't use it all the time when he walked. He preferred to trail it along walls. It was the cane, banging against the metal staircase that I'd heard as he approached.

Rick's favorite way of punishing someone was to get them down on the ground and then beat an arm or a leg with the cane until the bones were powder. And this was the man who basically owned my brother, in the kind of backroom "management" deal that involves no paper or ink, only handshakes and threats.

Alec could easily have taken him in a fight—maybe even with the cane. But Rick never went anywhere without his protection, two ex-heavyweight boxers called Al and Carl.

We turned. Rick was in his favorite gray suit with a blood-red shirt and silver tie. He always dressed classy, as if that could disguise what he was. His two bodyguards were right behind him.

"Am I interrupting something?" asked Rick. "That how it works in Holland? Brothers and sisters get....*close?*" He leered at us.

I wanted to kill him. Alec was the one thing I had left in the world. How could Rick take something so good and twist it into something perverted? I shook my head.

That was a mistake. With Rick, there never *was* any right answer. Whatever you did, it would end in pain or humiliation.

"I don't mind," said Rick. "If you want to kiss him for good luck. A good, big kiss on the lips."

I heard Alec's intake of breath. Normally, he tried to keep me away from Rick and I was happy to oblige. Coming down here had been a mistake.

I shook my head again.

"Rick—" started Alec. He tried to keep his voice level, but I could hear the anger there.

"*WHAT?*" screamed Rick and slammed his cane against the pipes beside Alec. Everyone, even his two bodyguards, jumped. The sound reverberated around the room for long seconds. God, his pupils were enormous. He was really coked up. "She should kiss someone, for good luck." He wasn't going to let go of the idea. "Maybe she should kiss *me*." And his thin lips twisted into what he called a smile.

Alec was standing close enough to me that I could feel him tense up. I knew he was getting ready to fly at Rick and I knew how that would end. But the idea of kissing Rick made me sick.

Rick stepped forward. Alec squared up to him. *Shit!* Rick was going to wind up beating him up, before the fight had even started. I had to do something.

Before any of them could stop me, I stepped forward and grabbed Rick's hand where it held his cane. His skin was cold and clammy, very different to Aedan's warm touch. Rick's eyes widened in surprise and I thought he was going to hit me. But then I gently lifted his hand, and the cane with it, towards my face, and he relaxed as he saw what I had in mind.

I brought the ugly, gaudy crystal head of the cane up to my mouth and kissed it softly, the facets sharp against my lips. When I looked up at Rick, he was grinning all over his face.

"There," he said. "See? She's got the idea."

Rick planted his cane back on the floor with a hard little rap. I winced. I couldn't imagine how painful that thing would be, against flesh and bone. "You can take this guy, right?" he asked Alec.

Alec was still having to restrain himself. "Sure," he said tightly. "No problem. He's a little guy. One good hit and he'll go down."

"Good, 'cause I got a lot of my own money on you, tonight," said Rick. "Make sure he goes down and stays down." Then, with a final leer at me, he was walking out into the pit to introduce the fight, his bodyguards trailing him.

Alec turned to me and pulled me into another hug.

"You sure about this?" I said. I didn't know why, but I was suddenly panicking. "There's still time to pull out."

Alec didn't answer, but I knew what he was thinking: *no, there isn't.* Even if we didn't need the money, you don't just walk out on one of Rick's fights. You did what you were told or you had your legs broken.

"I got this," said Alec. "He's just a little guy." He released me from the hug but I kept stubbornly holding him until the last second. Then, reluctantly, I tapped my fists against his like we always did, our good luck charm.

"I'll see you afterward," said Alec. "Go upstairs and watch. And stay the hell away from Aedan."

And then he was jogging out into the pit.

6

SYLVIE

The crowd had gone quiet as I climbed the stairs back up to the balcony. I could make out Rick's voice, telling them who they'd be watching. "From the land of tulips and dykes"—the crowd snickered—"undefeated in The Pit these last three weeks, *The Dutchman!*"

Alec and I had both been born right here in New York, but he had to make it sound good.

"And stepping up to take him on tonight, a challenger from Detroit—*Morgan!*"

I faltered on the stairs. That was weird. Normally, Rick had a whole spiel. Did that mean he didn't know this Morgan guy? What if he was dangerous?

I raced up the rest of the stairs, slipped through the crowd and leaned over the balcony to look. To my relief, Morgan didn't look like much at all. He was at least five years older than Alec, maybe more. And he didn't have Alec's muscle or his height. Maybe this would be alright after all.

The Pit didn't go in for niceties. The bell was an air horn, blown every three minutes to give the fighters a minute to recover. There was no grinning blonde in a bikini holding up round numbers and no medics on standby for injuries. Most important of all, there was no referee. The rules were simple: you fought until one of you couldn't get up.

The horn sounded and Alec went in fast and confident, swinging a heavy right hook. I think he meant to take out Morgan fast, before anything went wrong.

Almost immediately, it did.

Alec wasn't slow on his feet, but Morgan made him look like he was sleepwalking. Whenever Alec swung, Morgan was somewhere else. His punches weren't heavy, but they were lightning-fast and precise. Within a minute, Alec was sweating and off-balance, guarding his side where Morgan had hit his kidneys.

I could feel my chest tensing up with every hit my brother took. *Who the hell is this guy? Who's Rick put him up against?*

By the second round, Alec was starting to tire. He wasn't used to a small, nimble fighter. He couldn't turn fast enough, couldn't protect his sides when Morgan darted around him. And then a vicious kick to the back of the leg made him crumple and stagger. His hands went out for balance, leaving him exposed, and Morgan started punching him in the face. *One, two, three, four—*

Alec finally got his hands up, but he was reeling. He slumped back against the concrete wall, blood pouring from between his fingers.

My insides had clenched into a tight, hard knot. I could barely breathe.

In the next break between rounds, the difference between them was obvious: Alec had to hold himself up using the wall, wiping the blood from his eyes. Morgan was rock steady and untroubled—not taunting and whooping but not worried, either. Just a professional, doing a job.

Then he stripped off his tank top and I saw the tattoos. *Military* tattoos. Rick had put my brother in the ring with some ex-Army guy.

The next round started.

I bolted for the stairs.

7

SYLVIE

A l, one of Rick's bodyguards, was watching from the little side room. He held his arms out to block me, a solid wall of suited muscle.

"*Stop the fight!*" I screamed. "He'll kill him!"

He shook his head. "You know how it works. Crowd have paid their money. It's over when it's over."

When one of them can't get up. I could feel the bile rising in my throat. Behind Al, I could see Alec being driven back by a flurry of blows. His head rocked left, right, left. I imagined his brain being hammered inside his skull. All that delicate artistry that made him *him*: his personality, his kindness, his memories of our parents. It was being wiped out, punch by punch.

I launched myself at the pit. I'd throw myself between the two of them, if I had to. But then Al caught me easily around the waist and held me back. I stretched, clawing at the air, reaching for Alec. "*No!*"

The punches kept coming. Alec's legs went to jelly and he fell to his knees, his head lolling forward. *He's going to go down anyway. Stop, now! Stop! Please stop!*

Morgan didn't look cruel as he did it. He didn't gloat. He was just like Alec, trapped in the system Rick had created. But he needed to win, just as Alec had.

I remember screaming as he drew his arm back. Alec's eyes opened for a second and I thought he looked at me.

Then Morgan's fist smashed against the side of his head and he fell to the floor.

8

SYLVIE

There was no moment of victory for Morgan. Rick didn't come and hold his fist aloft and proclaim him the new champion. The crowd fell quiet—they could sense that things had gone very badly wrong. Rick's fighters weren't supposed to lose, not on their home turf. Especially when he'd been betting on them.

Morgan slunk past me with an apologetic glance. Al finally let me go and I ran to Alec's body. He was slumped on his back, his legs bent awkwardly. *Shit. Shit! Should I move him? Not move him? Is he breathing?* "ALEC!"

No response. But I could see a hint of movement in his chest. He was still alive—just.

The crowd was clearing out fast, now the entertainment was over. I heard the distinctive rattle and clang of Rick descending the stairs. As he approached, I spoke without looking up. "Have you called 911? We need to get him to the hospital...." I looked up, expecting to see...not *apology*, not from Rick. But concern. Regret.

What I got was something else altogether.

"*Wake up!*" screamed Rick. His cane sliced through the air and hit Alec's leg only a few inches from where my hand was resting. I heard the snap as the bone broke.

Alec jerked but didn't open his eyes. I flung myself instinctively off him and crawled to one side, my arms up to protect myself.

"You cost me twenty grand, you weak little fuck!" yelled Rick. Oh Christ—he was even more coked up than before.

My brain was trying to come to terms with what I was hearing. How could he blame *Alec?* But this was Rick. Someone else was always to blame.

"It—It wasn't his fault," I said, trying to keep my voice level. "The other guy was ex-Army or something. I saw the tattoo." I looked towards Alec. "Please, Rick—we have to get him to hospital."

Rick ignored my plea completely. He rounded on his bodyguards. "I *told* you to check that guy out!" he bawled to Al. "I *said* there was something wrong about him."

The bodyguards were smart enough to nod apologetically, even though I was betting they'd had no part in picking Morgan. More likely Rick had chosen him himself during a coke-fueled binge.

Alec's breathing was growing weaker. I crawled back to him and put my arms around his neck, drawing him close. *"Please, Rick!"*

"You think I'm letting him walk out of here?" Rick asked. He brandished his cane. "After what he cost me? I got another fight in a month and no one to put on!" He suddenly swung the cane down again, hitting Alec's ankle, this time. There was a sickening crunch.

I threw myself across my brother's legs. *"Please!* Please, no more!"

Rick's face darkened even more. He was angrier than I'd ever seen him. I saw, to my horror, that even his bodyguards were backing away. *He's out of control.* "You'd better move," he told me. "Unless you want this cane shoved up you."

I wasn't crying. I was too scared to cry. He was going to kill Alec. He was going to rip my one remaining piece of family away from me. *"Please!"*

"He's better off dead," said Rick. "If he can't fight, he's worthless to me." He twirled the cane and then raised it over his head. "Get the fuck out of the way."

I didn't know what to say. I couldn't move. I knew that me being there wouldn't stop him. I knew that he'd just swing that cane straight down and batter his way through me, again and again, until he hit Alec. But I couldn't leave my brother to die. I hugged Alec's legs and tensed my whole body, waiting for the pain to hit. I searched for something, anything, to say that would stop this. And as the cane whistled down, my brain finally came up with two words.

"*I'll fight!*" I screamed.

The end of the cane smacked into the concrete an inch from my head. For a few seconds, the only sound in the room was the eerie ringing of it.

"What?" asked Rick. He sounded genuinely puzzled.

I was still pressed against Alec's body. I could feel his breathing —*God, so weak*. I gingerly raised myself up and twisted around to face Rick. "I'll fight," I said again. This time, the words actually registered in my brain.

One of the bodyguards started to laugh.

"I'll fight, here in The Pit," I said. "Put me on instead of Alec. I'll fight whoever you want."

Rick looked at me with something between disgust and fascination. "*You?*" He looked at his two bodyguards for help. Al was laughing. Carl just looked amazed.

"Please," I said. Now the tears had started. I could feel them rolling down my cheeks. "Please. Let me—Let me fight."

Rick's forehead wrinkled. "A *girl* fight?"

"A catfight," said Al, grinning cruelly.

Rick considered. Then he lifted his cane and poked it under my chin. He used it to lift my head and turn it, examining me from all sides. I let him. "You've never fought in your life, have you?" he asked.

I shook my head.

He squatted down so that he was on my level. "That crowd up there wants *blood,*" he told me. "That isn't going to change, with two women. Whoever I get to fight you is going to beat the living crap out of you." He leaned closer. "*It goes on until someone can't get up.* You know what that means?"

I nodded slowly. Every loser got beaten unconscious, but death was always a risk. Even Alec had come out of this fight barely alive—

he still might die. For me—small, fragile and untrained—the ending would be inevitable.

If I lost, I was going to die.

I looked down at Alec. My tears were leaving dark, spreading pools on his tank top, mixing with the blood from his wounds.

"I understand," I said. "I'll do it. I'll fight."

9

AEDAN

I could have ridden the train all the way back to Newark. Hell, I could have gotten a cab—I was okay for money, since I didn't have much of anything to spend it on. But I like walking. No one bothers you, walking at night. Not if you look like me.

So I got off a few stops early and walked past the industrial parks and the docks, past walls of shipping containers taller than buildings and past black water as still and calm as glass.

My apartment block's lousy for just about everything—no nearby stores, no nightlife. Half the apartments are empty, some with broken windows. No one in their right mind would want to rent there. Which is exactly why I liked it. No neighbors, no visitors. Everyone left me alone.

Upstairs, I opened the windows to try to let in some air—the air conditioning broke a long time ago. But there was barely a breath of wind.

I settled for a shower, cranking the spray up hard and cold and letting it blast against my body, foaming and hissing against my chest and then my back. Cold showers were a boxing thing, a good way of helping swollen muscles to heal. I hadn't needed that for a long time. I'd kept in shape, still went to the same gym, but I hadn't felt that burn and ache that comes from really using your body. Working out isn't like fighting, in the same way cruising in your car on the freeway isn't like a race.

But tonight...tonight, I could feel just a hint of it. Just a touch of that fire in my shoulders and chest, from swinging punches. Just a little throb in my fists where they'd connected with those bastards faces.

It felt good. I tried to tell myself it was because I'd *done* good, because I'd saved Sylvie. But I knew it went deeper than that. *Fighting* had felt good.

It was the first time I'd raised my hands to anyone in over a year. The first time I'd let myself be myself, instead of a locked-down, hooded nobody.

And something else had felt good, too. Her. The sight of her; the touch of her. I squeezed my hand shut, remembering the feel of her soft skin against my calloused fingers. The scent of that long dark hair when it had passed close to my face, like walking through a fucking meadow filled with blossoms.

I turned off the shower and toweled myself dry. But the memories didn't stop.

The way her ripe breasts had pushed out the top of that pink t-shirt. The curve of her, from breast to waist, sculpted just perfectly for me to grab her and lift her and push her up against a wall.

I hit the light and flopped onto my bed, naked. It was way too hot for clothes. I lay there in the darkness with a faint breeze blowing in through the window.

Her back. That feline curve that ran from between her shoulders all the way down to the top of her ass. It made me want to strip her naked and run my palm down it. Maybe she'd gasp a little as the heel of my hand rubbed against that soft, tan skin, my fingers trailing along each sensitive vertebra.

Her legs. Those fantastic, sculpted calves and thighs, the tight denim hugging every smooth curve, leading up to—

I could feel my cock rising now, unbidden.

Her ass. Those tight, tight globes, high and firm and sticking out in just the right way. Just the right size for my hands to cup and squeeze. She'd groan. And then, with her on all fours, I'd gently part them....

My cock was pointing at the ceiling, now, throbbing. *No. For feck's sake!* I wasn't going to jack off to her like some teenager.

Her lips. Pink and full and so *soft.* Pressed together, a lot of the time, like she was worried about stuff. I wanted to take that away. I wanted to see her smile. The closest I'd seen was that little sigh of relief when she'd finally gotten her soda, and her lips had parted to show shining white teeth. It was burned into my memory: the little beads of sweat on her forehead, the way her lips had trembled when she paused her drinking and panted in air.

It was easy to imagine her on top of me: head thrown back, that long, silky hair flowing down her naked back and spilling over my hands. I'd be stroking her all the way from her ass up to her shoulders and my cock would be buried inside her, her thighs clamped around me. She'd pant and beg as she spasmed around me—

I snatched my hand away from my cock, thumped the pillow in frustration, and turned over on my side.

There was no use fantasizing about what I couldn't have. The worst thing in the world for Sylvie would be to get mixed up with a monster like me. I liked her—feck, I was hard as iron for her.

So I'd have to steer clear of The Pit.

For both our sakes, I'd make sure I never saw her again.

10

SYLVIE

There was a cab ride, paid for with the cash I dug from Alec's pockets. Then the blinding fluorescent lights of the hospital. Alec on his back on a gurney and doctors shouting questions at me as I ran alongside.

What happened?

Was he attacked?

Do you want us to call the cops?

And me lying and making up a story about him getting mugged in an alley and the guy taking a crowbar to his leg. *I didn't get a good look at him. It was dark. Please, just help him.*

I saw them looking at each other and at the cuts on Alec's knuckles—some new, some old. They didn't believe me. He wasn't the first bare-knuckle fighter to be brought in.

They talked about hemorrhaging and swelling and needing to relieve the pressure. One of them, before the others could stop him, demanded to know why I'd waited so long before bringing him in. I burst into tears.

They took him into emergency surgery, leaving me with a wad of forms to fill out. I went through them methodically, one by one, which took my mind off the horrors happening in the operating theater. Then I stared at the wall and tried to figure out how everything had gone so wrong, so fast.

~

After five hours, they said I could see him. Everything above his eyebrows was swathed in white bandages. When I saw the tube down his throat and the papery hiss and pump of the ventilator, I wanted to scream. His eyes were closed, but it didn't look like any sort of peaceful sleep. His brow was furrowed, as if he was having a nightmare.

One he couldn't wake up from.

"He's in a coma," said the doctor, taking a seat beside me. She was a pretty blonde who looked not much older than me. "That's not unusual, with head injuries. In some ways, it's the brain's way of protecting itself."

"While it heals, right?" I asked.

She just looked at me sadly.

"It'll protect him while he heals and then he'll wake up...right?" I pressed.

"There's no way to tell," she said slowly. "He *may* just wake up." But her face told me how unlikely that was.

I felt my lip tremble and then, without warning, I started weeping and couldn't stop. The doctor put a hand on my back and awkwardly patted me there. It felt as if it was the first time she'd done it—she really *was* young, I realized. But however awkward it was, I was glad she was there.

"Can I stay with him?" I croaked, when I could finally speak again.

"Of course." She gave me her beeper number and told me to call her any time.

When she'd gone, I sat there staring at Alec. My whole life, he'd been the big one, the strong one, the one who'd taken care of me...even while our parents had still been alive.

But cancer had eaten away at Mom until she was just a jaundiced, skeletal copy of herself in a hospice, and Alec had had to step up even more. Then we'd gotten the phone call to say something had happened to our dad at work. Alec had been the one who'd dealt with the doctors and then the funeral parlor. *Undiagnosed heart defect.* My brother had insisted I get my heart checked in case it was hereditary, and I'd demanded that he did, too. We were both clear. But now we were alone.

We'd clung to each other even closer, battling to keep the rent paid on the apartment. Our family's situation had been precarious even before Dad died—his savings had gone on Mom's cancer care. Every bill became a struggle.

And now, the person I'd leaned on so much was the one who needed help. He didn't look big or strong anymore. Surrounded by machines, dependent on them for every breath, he was more vulnerable than a newborn baby.

I picked up his hand and clasped it in mine. "I'm going to take care of you," I whispered. But I had no idea how. I had no money to pay the hospital bills. And in a month, I'd be dead at the hands of some trained fighter. With me gone, Alec would have no surviving relatives. *Jesus, they'll switch off the machine.*

I was going to die. And not long after that, Alec was going to die, too. I'd thought I was sacrificing myself for him, but all I'd done was to seal both our fates.

I wrapped my arms around him and hugged him tight, my face against his chest, my tears soaking into his hospital gown. I lost myself in a fantasy where his strong arms suddenly rose and tightened around me and he woke up and the doctors ran in and said *it's a miracle.* It would happen any minute, I told myself. I just had to keep hugging him.

But it didn't happen. My tears turned cold and the dawn crept slowly in through the blinds. Another day. One step closer to the end —a long month that I'd face utterly alone. And then, when it finished, I'd be dead.

I thought of the hard concrete floor of The Pit. My head cracking against it, blood spreading out in a pool. I hadn't given a lot of thought to the fight itself, until now. Back when I was pleading with Rick, it had seemed like a simple trade—my life for Alec's. But now, I started to think about how it would feel to be hit, again and again. No one had ever really hit me, my whole life. A few guys had groped me, a friend had slapped me, once. But no one had ever deliberately pulled back their fist and hit me. It was one thing my shitty life had spared me.

I was scared. I was scared of how much it would hurt. I imagined my cheekbones shattering, my ribs breaking. I was ashamed of how scared I was.

And it wasn't going to stop. I was going to be punched and kicked until I lost consciousness, until I slumped to the floor in a ragged heap. Even if I was still alive when the fight was over, there'd be no one to take *me* to the hospital. Maybe Rick would take pity on me and put me out of my misery, or maybe he'd just dump my body in an alley somewhere, but I'd be dead either way.

I clutched my brother tight, feeling the warmth of the sunlight crawl slowly across my back. It became uncomfortable, but I didn't want to move. Moving meant letting go of Alec and the beginning of the end. When it finally grew too hot to bear, I twisted and glared angrily at the window, one hand up in front of my eyes, dazzled by the new day.

And suddenly, in that second, I knew what I had to do.

I had to win.

That was the only way out. If I lost, we were both dead, one way or another. If I won, I'd survive. I'd be there for Alec and I could make sure he had the best chance, too.

But that meant fighting. Not just showing up like a sacrificial lamb and taking the punishment until I collapsed, but fighting some other woman and winning. I'd never been in a fight in my life.

I had to learn how to fight.

But where the hell was I going to learn that? Who was going to teach me? I didn't need some personal trainer in a gym. I needed someone *serious*. Someone who knew how to fight bare knuckle and raw. Someone who was a natural at this stuff. I didn't know anyone like that.

Wait.

I knew one.

11

AEDAN

M y place was close enough to the docks that the sound of engines and cranes woke me. It was almost comforting.

I didn't like being around people, ever since I'd quit fighting. It wasn't just the scars; it was the knowledge of what I'd become. At first, I told myself I was afraid of losing my cool and getting into a fight. I was staying in self-imposed solitary to protect other people. *Yeah, right.*

Deep down, I knew I was ashamed.

I sat up...and groaned. I could feel that bone-deep tiredness roll over me, the sort where you want to nod off every time you close your eyes. Not what I needed when I had to haul cargo around all day. Sure, these days the machines did most of the heavy lifting, but there was still plenty of raw muscle needed. Normally, I slept like a baby. Last, night, though....

Last night I'd been kept awake by visions of a dark-haired angel. They'd alternated between stupid, romantic fantasies of her in my arms and twisted nightmares where I hadn't been there to get her out of that bathroom at The Pit. I wanted to fuck her. I wanted to save her. I needed to be with her.

And I knew I'd never see her again.

I sighed, downed some coffee, and told myself to *grow the feck up*.

An hour later, I was helping load a container onto a truck when my radio blared. It pissed me off a little, because you don't want any distractions when you've got tons of steel hanging above your head. "What?" I snapped into my handset.

It was Aggie, the matronly redhead who worked the front gate. "One of your women," she told me. It sounded even more disapproving in her bored, north-Jersey accent.

I ran a hand over my face. It wasn't like I had a string of girls coming to see me at work. Hell, I hadn't slept with anyone in months. But I'm not a feckin' monk, either. There'd been a few hook-ups in Newark bars, and once or twice I'd been dropped off at work by a Sandy or a Mandy or a Cindy the next morning...I wasn't even sure which had been which, now. It had just been empty sex, though it had taken the edge off. And Aggie had seen, and that had given me a reputation.

Well, *feck her*. I never claimed to be a good guy.

"Which one?" I asked tiredly.

"I'm not your secretary, Aedan," she snapped.

I let out a long sigh and gestured for the crane to lower a little. *"Aggie!"*

She swore under her breath and I heard her bark out the question to whoever was waiting at the gate. "Sylvie," she snapped.

And time seemed to stop.

The next thing I knew, Dwight was bawling down at me from the crane, *"Hey! Down or up or what, ya idiot?"* and Aggie was on the radio again and I realized I'd been standing there gaping for about a minute.

She looked even smaller than I remembered her. Small and slender, even with that firm ass and those cute, pert breasts. But it was more than that, something in the way she held herself. She looked *fragile*.

I'd taken a break to go talk to her, which meant I wouldn't get another one until lunch. Worse was the interrogation I'd get from Aggie, later.

I walked Sylvie out to the edge of the dock, where you could look out across the water towards Manhattan. A few gulls were circling overhead. "How did you find me?" was my first question.

"I called around—people my brother knew at The Pit. Everyone's heard of Aedan. You're a freaking legend. One of them said they thought you worked at the docks."

I looked around at the little slice of industrial hell where I worked. "There are a lot of places around the docks. How'd you know it was this one?" It came out angrier than I intended. I'd just got used to my quiet little life there. It felt like she was bringing that whole world of blood and glory back into my life, and I didn't want it. Or maybe I wanted it so badly it freaked me out.

"I didn't know." She lifted her chin. "This is the tenth place I've asked at."

Jesus. The poor girl must have been walking around Newark all morning. I had to admire her determination. "Why?"

She looked me right in the eye. "I need you to teach me how to fight."

It was so unexpected, so utterly ridiculous, that I couldn't help but laugh. I didn't want to offend her—seeing her there, dark hair blowing in the breeze, was easily the best thing that was going to happen to me for months. But the idea of her swinging her fists....

"Don't laugh at me," she said, stiffening.

"I'm...I'm not," I said, trying to control it. I shook my head. "It's just...." I sighed and felt myself grin. The idea was cute. "Look. Go to your gym, find a trainer." I didn't mean it to sound patronizing, but a little of that tone crept in. "They'll teach you how to hit a bag—"

"I don't mean that," she said coldly. "I mean in The Pit. I need to learn to fight like you."

I frowned at her. "*Why?* Why would you even—"

She told me what had happened after I'd left. The deal she'd made with Rick. My grin vanished and I stared at her in horror. *Jesus, Mary and Joseph...*she was going to get killed. The idea of my dark-haired angel lying broken on that concrete floor made me want to throw up.

"Run," I said. "Get a bag and leave town."

"I can't. My brother's here and I can't move him from the hospital. If I don't show up, Rick'll take it out on him."

She was right. That cruel bastard would think nothing of sending someone to finish off the poor guy. Hell, all they'd have to do was flip a switch on a machine. And going to the police wasn't an option— Rick had enough money and a greasy enough lawyer that he'd walk unless he was caught red-handed.

"You know him, don't you?" she asked. "You know what Rick's like. You were a fighter, once."

I stared at her.

"A lot of people had stories, when I started asking around. An Irish fighter called Aedan who wiped the floor with *everyone*. They said you were undefeated for almost a *year!*"

I shook my head. "That was a long time ago. I don't fight anymore."

"Please," she said, and the sound of that word on her lips made my heart melt. Oh, Jesus, I would have given her anything she wanted, right at that moment. Anything at all.

Anything but that.

"Please," she said again. "He's my brother. I can't run and leave him behind. He's the only family I've got. Do you know what that's like?"

I closed my eyes and thought of my own brothers. A very different situation, but no less painful.

I rubbed my back, right between my shoulder blades. "Yeah," I said. "I do."

Her face filled with hope. "So you'll help me?" She stepped forward a little and I could smell the scent of her—honeysuckle shampoo and soap and a warm, fragrant spice that was just *her*. She was gorgeous, so beautiful that it took my breath away just to look at her. And she needed me. I could sweep in like some knight on a white feckin' horse and rescue her.

Except I'm no hero.

I thought about going back to that world. Violence and fear. Glory and excitement. The wonderful savagery of it, the way it changed you. I thought about raising my hands to someone again, and I felt ill. I thought about raising my hands to *her*, even in training, and my guts twisted.

"No," I said. And turned away.

12

SYLVIE

I'd very nearly not come. Alec's warning was still ringing in my head. He'd wanted me to stay away from Aedan because he was dangerous, a legendarily brutal fighter. And yet the irony was, *brutal* was exactly what I needed, right now. *Brutal* might just save my life.

But Alec had started to say something else, too, just before the fight. He'd been scared for me. *"The guy's a real bastard. I heard—"*

What? What had he heard? All I'd gotten out of people at The Pit was vague impressions, no details. But they all agreed he was a great fighter...and someone to stay the hell away from.

Instead of staying away, I'd come all the way out to Newark, alone, and sought him out. Because I really didn't have any choice. And because I'd thought I'd seen something in him, back at The Pit. I thought I'd glimpsed someone, underneath the hardness and the scars. Someone who might just be able to save me.

The way he made me feel only made it worse. Seeing him in daylight, that combination of rugged good looks and raw power was even more acute. He was gorgeous, but not in any familiar, safe way, like the guys I saw around the city. He didn't belong in New York, with its rules and its civility. He'd have been at home a thousand years in the past, back in Ireland, defending his home from an invading army, bellowing a war cry as he tossed men over his shoulder. It made perfect sense that he'd wound up in The Pit, the most barbaric place the city had to offer.

He should have scared me—he still *did* scare me, in a way. But every time I looked into those eyes, I felt like I was falling. Every time I watched his lips move, I felt the ghost of their imagined touch on mine. That accent was the most wondrous thing I'd ever heard, a complex melody of flowing vowels and upward lilts. It was music made from dirty steel and slabs of stone and it did a number on me every time he spoke.

And then he'd said the one word I hadn't expected: *no.* The word washed over me and seeped into my skin, chilling it like a north wind. I took a half step back, stumbling as if he'd slapped me.

Maybe Alec had been right about him. Maybe he really was a bastard.

And it was worse than that. I'd got it into my head, somehow, that he liked me. I was sure I'd felt his eyes on me, more than once. The shame rose up in my stomach, hot and wet and flaring scarlet. *Of course he doesn't like you.* A super-hot guy like *him?* From the way the woman at the gate glared at me, I wasn't the first woman to come looking for him. Maybe he'd taken a passing interest in me, considered me for a casual fuck, but nothing more than that.

When he'd helped me, back at The Pit, it had been out of pity, or because he felt he had no choice. And now I'd showed up at his work full of expectations and he just wanted rid of me.

I hated him, in that moment. I felt like the geeky girl who smiled shyly at the football captain and heard the whole room collapse into laughter. All I wanted to do was walk away.

But I couldn't. I still needed him. There was no one else who could help me.

I couldn't bribe him—I didn't have any money.

There was only one thing I could offer him instead.

13

AEDAN

"You can have me."

Her voice was sullen and desperate, close to tears. It took me a few seconds to really process what she'd said.

When I spun around, she was lifting the hem of her tank top. A sleek, tan stomach came into view, then the purple cups of her bra. The tank top pulled tight across her breasts and she hooked it over them. Soft, sweet perfection, the flesh bouncing lightly as it was freed. Everything I'd dreamed of....

"You can have me," she said again. "I'll sleep with you." She was staring right at me, her eyes brimming with tears. "Just—*please*—teach me how to fight."

I broke out of the spell she'd cast on me and stepped quickly over to her. Grabbing her tank top, I rammed it down again, covering her. Trying not to think about how smooth her skin was, how good it felt as it grazed my fingers.

I stood there panting with the shock of it. I glanced around. No one else was nearby, thank God. "Jesus!" I snapped. "What are you *doing*?"

She looked up at me and blinked a couple of times. I could see the tears start to spill. *Oh feck!* Now she thought I didn't want her.

She folded her arms protectively over her stomach, hugging the tank top to her. "I'm sorry," she sobbed. "It's all I have left. What do you want? What will it take?"

Oh Jesus! What have I done?! I felt as if Dwight had dropped the damn cargo container right on me, crushing me down into the dirt. I'd reduced her to this. I'd made this angel want to trade her body like a whore because I was too ashamed to go back to—

I can't. I really can't. She's a girl! And I was a fighter, not a trainer. Even if I could train her, how much good could I do, in a month?

I stared at her hopelessly. Her face was upraised to me, the tears coursing down her cheeks. I'd never seen anyone look so vulnerable. A single word from me, now, and she'd crumble completely.

She has no one else to go to. If she did, she wouldn't be here.

And what was the alternative? Turn her away and know that she was going into that fight without any preparation at all? I knew that I'd never be able to persuade her to run. She felt the same way about her brother as I did about—

I felt the tattoo on my back itch.

"Okay," I said at last. "But you don't need to...do that."

She didn't say anything. She was too busy trying to hold back the tears. She closed her eyes and nodded twice, sniffing.

I felt my stomach clench. She was going to feel grateful. She'd want to reward me. Even if she didn't really like me, she'd offer up the temptation. That face. That body. Every feckin' day. And I'd have to keep pushing her away because the best way to hurt her would be to let her get involved with me. She wasn't like one of the women I'd picked up in bars. She deserved better than me.

It had to be all business. Just training.

I took a deep breath. "We start tomorrow."

14

SYLVIE

I agonized about what to wear. It wasn't like I had a massive collection of gym wear to choose from—when I did exercise, it was a clumsy attempt to follow an aerobics video I'd found on YouTube, in the privacy of my bedroom with the blinds closed. So all I had was sweatpants and Lycra tops.

The problem, as I was hotly and painfully aware, was that Aedan would be there. And however much I was focused on the fight, however scared I was for Alec and myself and what awaited us in a month's time, I couldn't stop thinking about him. I knew his reputation. I knew I should be running in the opposite direction. But instead, I kept thinking about the feel of his hand on mine, when he'd briefly held it. Those blue eyes that seemed to see everything. The jagged, ugly scars on his neck that only made the rest of him seem more beautiful. *I should be scared of him.* I *was* scared of him. But at the same time, I was drawn to him. And so I agonized about what to wear.

Eventually, I screamed at my own reflection in the mirror. And I stood there, listening to the silence and, after a few seconds, I realized I'd been waiting for Alec's answering shout from his room, telling me to shut up. That nearly started me crying again.

It had been a long night. I'd slept alone in the apartment plenty of times, of course—Alec had had plenty of one-night stands, usually with curvy blondes, and he preferred to go back to their place because no one wants to have to introduce their sister over breakfast. But I'd always known, those times, that he'd be coming back eventually.

I threw a towel in a bag and headed out before I could think about it anymore.

~

The gym wasn't what I'd expected. It didn't look much like the gyms I'd seen on TV, all polished wood floors and gleaming machinery and sunlit, airy studios filled with people doing yoga.

This was a boxer's gym.

The walls were whitewashed breezeblocks. There were only two types of equipment: things to lift and things to hit. And the place was full of men lifting and hitting.

That was the other thing that was missing: women. I couldn't see a single woman in the entire place. I stood there feeling completely out of place.

Then an Irish voice from behind me. "You okay?"

For a moment, I thought it was Aedan. I spun around and found myself looking at someone completely new. He was a little smaller in the shoulders than Aedan and leaner, too, though he was ripped as hell. And he was topless. A tattoo on his bicep said *Ruth*. A fresher-looking one on his other bicep said *Karen*.

He had blue-gray eyes and similar black hair to Aedan. Almost as good looking, too. What was this? Had I stumbled into some Irish-run gym? Was it a membership requirement that you be blue-eyed and gorgeous? "Umm..."

"Relax," he told me. "You aren't the only woman."

I looked around. "No?"

"Oh, no. Natasha's been here. And Jasmine." He frowned and then gave me a look that managed to be flirty and apologetic at the same time. "To be fair, they only came *once,* but..."

"Making friends?" Another Irish voice, behind me. One that sent an unexpected tremor of excitement down my spine. I spun again to see Aedan. He was in a blue tank top and black sweatpants and he looked...amazing. The other guy was ripped and good looking in a filthy sort of a way. But Aedan was powerful on a different level—raw and primal. *Dangerous.* If the other guy was a wolf, Aedan was a lion. And he was staring at the other guy with a knowing glare and just a hint of...*something.*

"Just saying hi," said the other guy, grinning. He looked between the two of us questioningly.

"I'm training her," said Aedan. And there was something in the way he said it, something that made me frown inside. As if there was an unspoken message alongside it.

"Oh," said the other guy, nodding as if *message received.* "Okay. No problem. Got it." And he gave Aedan an especially big grin.

Aedan put an arm around my waist and led me away. "Don't mind Connor," he muttered. "The fecker just...flirts."

"Was he? Did he?" For some reason, I was blushing. I was also trying not to react to the feel of Aedan's muscled arm caressing my waist with each step. I was re-running the conversation in my head. Had he just basically told Connor to back off?

Was Aedan *jealous?*

Aedan must have caught my confused look because he cleared his throat and shrugged. "He's just some wanker," he muttered. "Plays the guitar and thinks women all worship the ground he walks on. Flirts even now that he's attached."

I nodded to let him know I understood. But my mind was spinning. He *was* a little jealous. And, at the same time, I was trying to keep a straight face because I'd never heard anyone say *wanker* before.

He led me over to a thick gym mat and slipped off his sneakers. It hit me just how big the size difference was between us. It wasn't just his height—it was the width of his muscled shoulders and the *presence* of him. He looked like a statue made out of granite. I felt as if I was made out of matchsticks.

This is ridiculous. I can't learn how to fight. Look at me!

But it was the only chance I had.

I knelt to untie my sneakers. I'd settled, in the end, for gray sweatpants and a black Lycra top over a sports bra. As I knelt there, I became aware of something. A sort of hot, tingling wave lashing across the tops of my breasts. A feeling that soaked down into me and finished between my thighs.

I didn't have to look up to know he was staring down at me. It only lasted a second. When I glanced up, he was looking off towards the far end of the gym. *Maybe I imagined it.* Maybe I was just transferring all my feelings onto him.

I couldn't take my eyes off his shoulders. Under the hooded top, they'd looked big. Now, though, exposed by the tank top, they were huge—powerful and solid, and the way his arms narrowed and then flared again into thick biceps and sculpted forearms...*wow.* I'd been expecting him, somehow, to be covered in tattoos—a lot of fighters were. But I couldn't see one anywhere. The only mark on him was that jagged, twisting maze of scars down one side of his neck. I could see it better, in the daylight, and the viciousness of it made my chest ache. Someone had not just stabbed him but twisted and gouged and —*Jesus.* What would drive someone to do that to him?

It didn't make him ugly—not in my eyes. It made me want to kiss him, there, press my lips along every hardened scar. If my kisses couldn't heal him, they could at least show him that it didn't matter.

That isn't going to happen. Going by his gruff manner, this was going to be all business, even if he *had* been a little jealous when he saw Connor talking to me.

That knowledge didn't stop me looking, though. It couldn't—his body was too damn addictive, harder and more solidly *real* than any guy I'd seen. His strong chest narrowed to a trim waist, giving him that gorgeous X shape between shoulder and thigh. *Big* thighs, too. Powerful. And between them—

I jerked my eyes upward and found myself looking right into his.

He'd been staring down at me again, just as my eyes had strayed towards his cock. I didn't know which of us was more embarrassed.

I slipped off my sneakers and stood up. "Okay," I said. "Where do we start?"

He nodded, all business again. I was getting all kinds of mixed signals from this guy. Did he like me or not? And it didn't help that, up close to him like this, he was freaking intimidating. That darkness, rolling off him in waves. The sense that, without even thinking about it, he could just crush your head or pound you into the ground.

Pound me into the ground. The phrase echoed around my head a few times and then seeped mockingly down into my body, liquid-hot. I forced myself to focus, my face growing hot, and looked expectantly up at him.

"Hit me," he said. That strong accent again, each short word like an impact of stone on metal. Harsh and uncompromising. And sexy as hell. *Hit him?!*

I blinked at him a couple of times. "Really?"

"Really."

I hesitantly made a fist and lifted it, then put it back down. "Just...hit you?"

"Just hit me."

I punched him lightly in the stomach, like I was miming it. My knuckles brushed his abs and I could feel the ridged hardness there, warm through the fabric.

"No...*actually* hit me. I have to see what you've got. Hit me like you mean it."

I swallowed and hit him as hard as I could, in the same spot. I expected him to do some lightning-fast block or maybe dodge out of the way. But he just stood there and my fist connected. I hit a wall of solid, warm muscle, like punching rubber. He rocked back maybe half an inch.

"Oh *shit!*" I said. "I'm so sorry!" I instinctively put my hand on his stomach where I'd hit him. "Are you okay?"

He looked down at my hand, then into my eyes. "Aye," he said softly.

I removed the hand.

He checked there was space behind him. "Come at me again," he said. "Try and hit me."

"Where?" I asked hopelessly.

"Anywhere."

He started to move backward in an easy, fast-footed shuffle. I swung at him and, this time, he moved. I missed completely. I tried again and he dodged the other way. He seemed to know where I was going to go before I did it. How was that possible?

He stopped suddenly and I pulled up short to avoid crashing into him. Then he lunged forward.

I yelped and staggered back, tripped over my own feet and went down. I landed with a *whump* on the mat, arms and legs everywhere. I instinctively glanced around the gym. Everyone else there looked like they belonged. Even Connor was slugging a punchbag. No one was actually laughing at me, but I could feel it in their looks. *What's* she *doing here?*

"Don't mind them," said Aedan. He put out his hand for me to take. "You've got as much right to be here as them."

I took his hand and he pulled me to my feet. His warm grip felt amazing. As if he could have easily lifted me right up into the air one-handed.

I wound up standing very close to him, our toes almost touching. For just a second, everything seemed to stop. My breathing quickened. We were close enough that the tips of my breasts were almost brushing his chest—

He stepped back and ran a hand through his hair. "You can't hit," he said. "You've got no feckin' power. You've got no idea how to stand or move or guard."

I stared at him, open-mouthed. "Well...*thanks.*"

But he hadn't finished. "You've got no balance," he said, shaking his head. "You've got no *presence.*"

"What the hell does *that* mean?" I asked angrily.

"You intimidate too easily. I got in your face and you jumped back."

I felt like I should deny it, but I knew he was right. "Is there anything *good?*" I asked at last.

He stared at me for much longer than the question deserved. His eyes roamed down my body from head to toe and I felt it as a hot wave again, sluicing deep down into me and finishing with a tightening at my groin. The air seemed to thicken and crackle between us.

"You're small," he said at last, looking at the floor. "That makes you harder to hit."

He lifted his eyes and we stared at one another.

"Well, that's something," I whispered.

He stared at me for three more beats of my racing heart...and then he sighed and glanced away. "Come on," he said. "Let's start with your stance."

He came around to stand behind me, so close that I could feel the heat of his breath on my neck. His big, warm hands landed on my shoulders and he started to guide me into the position he wanted me in.

The position he wanted me in. A shudder went through me. *Oh, quit that you moron! He doesn't even like you!* Or if he did, he was shying away from it for some reason.

None of which stopped his hands feeling absolutely amazing.

"You're right-handed, yeah?" he asked. I nodded. "Okay. Turn sideways a little. Makes you a smaller target. Left hand up like this— no, other way around." He gently turned my forearm. His big paws encircled it completely. "Other hand up like *this.*" Then his hands were sweeping down my sides to my hips. "The power has to come from here—understand? *Twist.*"

He left his hands there, the heat of him throbbing into me. I realized he was waiting for me to try it. I twisted, lashing out with my right hand, and felt my muscles move under his palms. Much like I was riding him and he was holding onto me as I writhed.

I nodded. "Got it," I said shakily.

He released his hands. But he seemed to do it almost reluctantly.

We practiced the boxer's shuffle, dancing back and forth with my weight over my back foot in case someone tried to kick the front one out from under me. I quickly learned how tiring just moving around the ring non-stop is—all those fast little movements add up. Then he put gloves on me for the very first time. I stared down at my hands with their huge, comedy padding. I felt like a mascot at Disneyland who'd forgotten the rest of her costume.

He showed me how to jab and cross and hook. After an hour, I felt like it was actually beginning to come together. I looked, if you squinted hard, kind of like a boxer. But he was looking at me with concern. It started to drive me crazy.

"What?" I demanded at last.

"You're too mechanical. Like a puppet with someone yanking your strings. You're just repeating what I've shown you."

"Of course I am! That's what you said to do!"

"But it's too...*stilted*. You're punching and moving. You're not *fighting*."

I looked at the bag we were hitting. "That's because I'm hitting a bag," I said, a little defensively.

"But in your head, you're not fighting. It's not coming from the heart."

I'd had enough. I was hot. I was exhausted. I was irrationally pissed off with him because I'd mistakenly thought I'd felt something between us. I remembered how I'd agonized over my clothes that morning and I wanted to shoot myself in the head. As if he'd even notice what I was wearing.

My hands were sweating in the gloves. I went to take one of them off so that I could hurl it down on the mat in frustration and discovered that it's almost impossible to un-velcro one glove while the other one's still on. "Goddamnit!" I yelled. "I'm trying! How about some positivity?"

His foot suddenly hooked under my ankle—I'd forgotten to keep my weight off of it. I fell backwards onto the mat for the second time that day, landing with a surprised grunt. Then he was on top of me, his hands pinning my shoulders to the mat.

"*Do you think* she's *going to go easy on you?*" he yelled. "Do you think she's going to care that you're a girl and a rookie? She's going to treat you like any other fighter!"

I looked up at him with huge eyes. It suddenly clicked that I hadn't been the only one getting frustrated over the last hour. He'd just been hiding it better. And now I could see the worry in his eyes. That was where the frustration was coming from: concern.

Concern for *me*.

"Sorry," I said quietly.

We stared at each other for a moment longer, and then the reality of our situation sank in. His knee was between my legs, pushing up against my groin through a few layers of cotton. His palms were resting on my bare shoulders and my breasts were heaving from the shock of falling. The air seemed as thick as honey. I could feel the sweat on my skin, making it glossy and slick under his hands.

I saw his eyes flick down to...my lips? *God, is he about to—*

15

AEDAN

I released her and stood up quickly. I had to put some distance between us or I was going to—*Christ, I nearly snogged her!*

I stood there staring down at her. *Feck,* she looked amazing. When I'd first seen her talking to Connor, I'd stood behind her for a while just gazing at that outfit before I interrupted them. Every time she'd moved, the sweatpants had pulled tight over her ass and I'd felt my cock twitch in my pants.

And then she'd been lying under me, sweating and open-mouthed, her lips just slightly trembling in that way they did. And just for a second—

Just for a second, I'd been weak.

"Sorry," I said. "I'm a shitty teacher."

"Well, I'm a lousy pupil," she said. "So I guess we match."

I hesitantly reached out my hand. She grabbed it and pulled herself up. God, she weighed nothing at all. How could I be doing this? How could I be even thinking about sending her into The Pit?

Because without me, she'd have no chance at all.

She stood up straight, dusting herself down, and her breasts bounced in a way that made my cock throb against my thigh. Then she shook back her hair and gave me a worried little smile, and I thought my heart was going to explode. God, I was hardwired to this woman. Every little thing she did sent a charge right through my brain. The rest of the world didn't seem to exist when she was around, the clang of metal weights and the slap of glove against bag becoming so much distant background hum. All that mattered was her.

And it was only getting worse, the more I was around her.

"I don't want to see you get hurt," I blurted, before I was really aware I was going to say it.

"Well then I guess we better get back to training." She looked up at me, challenging me. Feck me, I *wasn't* imagining it. She *was* into me. And I couldn't allow myself to do a damn thing about it. It was more than just not wanting to hurt her, now. If something happened between us and it went wrong and she ran, I wouldn't be able to help her.

"We should work on your power," I said. "Let's test your strength. See where you're at now, so we've got a baseline."

I showed her over to a weights bench, trying to keep my eyes off her ass. I got her to lie down on her back, then laid a barbell across the supports. I walked around behind her head so I could spot for her, grabbing the weight if she needed me to.

"Just do your best," I said. I was trying to be more patient, now, cursing myself for getting frustrated before. It wasn't her fault she was starting from scratch. Hell, she was doing a lot better than me, the first time I ever walked into a gym.

She set her jaw and lifted the barbell out of the supports, then lowered it down to her chest. She lifted it back up and racked it again —easily, because I'd started her out super-light. I figured she needed a win. "Good!" I said, with maybe a little too much enthusiasm.

She gave me a look. "What was that—five pounds? Don't patronize me."

I nodded, chastened. This teaching stuff was hard. I added another ten pounds. "Try that."

She lifted and lowered, steely-eyed. I added more weight. Christ, she might be little but she was determined. As I watched her grunt and push, I started to see beyond the obvious. I was in the perfect position, standing there, to stare right down her top at those gorgeous breasts. But I found myself looking at...*her*. The whole her. Looking at her and thinking how bloody unfair it was that she'd wound up here. I didn't know what had happened to get her into such a shitty situation. No one fights at The Pit unless they're desperate for money.

Well, not unless they're me.

Something must have gone really wrong in her life. She seemed smart and organized and she was driven as hell. She should have been studying to be a lawyer or something and instead she was preparing to fight for her life. It wasn't right.

She inhaled, then blew it out and pushed the bar up again. It was heavily loaded now, a real struggle for someone her size. Teeth gritted, forearms shaking, she heaved it up towards the top of its path. I put my hands gently under the bar in case her arms gave way.

"Don't...fucking...help me!" she managed.

"I'm not," I said. And I wasn't—my fingers were just barely brushing the underside of the bar. "It's all you."

She pushed...and *pushed* and got it back up onto the supports. She lay there panting and grinning in satisfaction. It was the first time I'd really seen her smile and *damn,* the sight of it hit me right in the chest. Then she caught my eye and I found myself grinning, too.

Smiling wasn't something I did often. I'd forgotten how good it felt.

16

SYLVIE

Aedan told me to grab a shower, because he was taking me to lunch. This being a man's gym, the women's changing room was kind of an afterthought, grudgingly added in what might well have been a former broom closet. The sign on the door said WOMAN and I wasn't sure if that was because they'd misspelled it or because they really didn't want to encourage women to show up in numbers and dilute the testosterone.

The shower worked, though, and soon I was in the street clothes I'd brought with me, hurrying along the street beside Aedan. "When you say *lunch,*" I said, "you mean, like...a coffee, right?" I was watching him carefully, alert for any sign of that smile coming back. When he'd grinned down at me by the weights bench, it had felt like my whole world had brightened. The memory was burned into my mind —the white teeth, that full lower lip, the way his cheeks dimpled...when he smiled, he went from broodingly handsome to drop-dead gorgeous. I wanted—*needed*—to see that smile again, because it was proof that I was right—that there was something gentler hiding underneath the muscles and scars.

"I mean *lunch.*"

"But it's only just noon! I'm not hungry yet." I normally didn't eat lunch for another hour or two, maybe grabbing a sandwich if I remembered.

"You're in training, now. You need protein." He turned to look at me. "We need to get some meat on those"—he stared at my arms, then at my legs, which took longer—"bones."

He showed me into a diner that was practically next door to the gym. The walls were covered in photos, many of them black and white. Every one of them showed a boxer.

"Aedan?" A waitress in her fifties bustled over to us. "Aedan, my sweet Irish boy." She gave him a hug. "We don't see you in here enough. And who's *this?*" She gave me an appraising look, which was roughly comparable to being inside an MRI scanner for an hour.

"Just someone I'm helping," Aedan told her. "Could you do us a couple of your boxer's breakfasts?"

She showed us over to a booth, grinning the whole time. When she'd left, I asked, "Your mother?"

"No. She just thinks she is."

"What's a *boxer's breakfast?*"

"You'll find out."

I looked at him across the blue and white tablecloth. "Where *is* your mom?" Then I paused. "I mean, if you don't mind me asking."

He looked at me. "I do."

"You do mind me asking?"

He nodded.

I felt crushed. "Oh. Sorry."

He sighed and shook his head. "*I'm* sorry. It's just something I don't talk about." He looked at me and then around at the room. "And I'm not good at...this."

"Lunch?"

"Talking." He rubbed his face and then gave a wry smile. "I've got a brother, Carrick. *He's* the talker. He'd talk your knickers right off."

"He wouldn't," I said quickly. Because, weirdly, just the idea of it felt like cheating.

"He would." And then he looked uncomfortable, as if he'd said too much. We descended into an uneasy silence. *Great, now I've pissed him off. He hates me.*

17

AEDAN

Great, now I've pissed her off. She hates me. I hadn't meant to shut down the conversation. But my family was one thing I couldn't talk about. I should never have mentioned my brother.

And then it got worse.

A hand slapped down on my shoulder. There's a certain way that cops do that, to let you know who's boss. And there was only one cop who'd have the guts to walk up and do it to me.

"Hi, Charlie," I said tiredly.

He stepped around to the side so that I could see him. He was barely taller than Sylvie—barely taller than *me*, sitting down. I'd never understood how he got past the academy's height requirements. Maybe he'd stood on a box the entire time. "How you doing?" he asked, which is cop-speak for *are you keeping your nose clean?*

"Good," I said. "Sylvie, Charlie. Charlie, Sylvie."

Charlie eyed our clothes. "You training again?" His jaw tightened. "Back at The Pit?"

"No. Teaching." I looked at Sylvie.

"Yeah," she said, picking up on my look. "Like a personal trainer. Boxercise."

Charlie stared at us just long enough to let us know that he didn't buy it for a second. Then he nodded. "Stay out of trouble." And, with another pat on the shoulder, he walked off.

Sylvie waited until he'd gone. "Who's *that* guy?"

"Someone I did a favor for, once."

"He doesn't seem all that grateful."

I winced. "He kind of repaid that debt, already."

To my relief, the food arrived. A generous steak and two eggs, sunny-side up.

Her eyes bulged. "Are you *kidding me?* You eat that for lunch?"

"No," I said seriously. "This is breakfast. We're catching up."

"I don't eat that much meat in a *week!*" she squeaked.

I furrowed my brow. "What *do* you eat?"

She shrugged. "Noodles. And a lot of breakfast cereal."

I sighed. "You're in training now. We need to build up your body. *Real* food."

She eyed her steak. "I can't afford this much *real food.*"

"I'm paying." And then, because she still looked doubtful, I blurted, "I'll pay for your meals."

She stared at me as if I'd offered her a ruby necklace. "Thank you," she said at last. She looked down at her food as she started to eat, but she kept glancing up at me as if I was the second coming.

Jesus, no one's ever given her a present before? No one's ever done anything nice for this girl? What the *feck* were all those other guys thinking? She should be getting real presents—dresses and jewelry and a feckin' Mercedes with a bow tied round it on her birthday. And all that romantic stuff—chocolates and flowers and those stupid scented soaps and candles that women like so much. She shouldn't be getting excited about some free meals.

"I don't get you," she said, frowning. When she frowned, she wrinkled her nose like a rabbit and I wanted to pull her out of her seat and snog her so bad. "One minute you're riding me about how badly I'm doing. The next you're being nice to me."

I looked down at my plate. "Just trying to do the right thing," I mumbled.

I could feel her eyes burning into me. "So, do you have many brothers?" she asked.

"Lots," I said. I thought of the tattoo on my back, as if it was glowing through my t-shirt.

"Where are they?"

"Around."

"Around New York?"

"Around America." I knew I was being cagey so I tried to turn it back to her. "It must be weird, living with your brother."

She nodded, her mouth full. Given that she'd said she wasn't hungry, she was wolfing down the steak and eggs. I wondered how long it was since someone had given her a decent meal.

When she eventually swallowed, she said, "He can get a little overprotective, if I bring a guy back. It's cute." She smiled for a moment and then it crumbled. She must have remembered where her brother was. *Ah, hell.*

"Does that happen a lot, recently?" The words were out before I could snap my mouth shut. *Shit!* Had I just sort-of-kind-of asked if she was single?

She looked up at me. "No. Not recently."

I could almost feel it throb in the air between us, like a heat haze. It wasn't just my imagination. She *did* like me. Which was bad, because I liked her even more.

She poked at her steak. "Paying for my meals is nice. Thank you."

"You're welcome."

But she wasn't finished. "I didn't know stevedores made that much money, though."

We didn't. I shrugged.

"And you don't fight anymore, right? So you're not making it that way. So what is it?" She leaned forward. "Are you smuggling stuff into the country? Like in *The Wire?*"

I stiffened. "Not all dock workers are on the take." I knew it was a shitty job, but it was *my* shitty job.

"Okay, sorry. So what is it? You're a secret millionaire?"

"It's only steak and eggs."

"Yeah, but you didn't even think about it. You just paid for it, and said you'd pay for my meals while we trained, which by the way I'm not even sure I'm totally comfortable with. I agonize for an hour over whether I can afford laundry detergent."

I leaned forward, putting my forearms on the table. It creaked. "You're annoyingly sharp."

"Why, thank you. So what's the secret income? Drugs? Are you a part-time gigolo?"

I sighed. "I don't earn any extra money. I just don't spend it."

She seemed taken aback. "Oh." Then, "Really?"

"Really."

"You mean you don't get out much?"

"*Look—*" And then I didn't know what to say. It had all been going so well, back at the gym. Slow progress, true, but she'd been trying really hard. And now suddenly, as soon as we'd got to the diner, everything had changed. I felt antsy and off-balance.

And then I realized what it was: I wasn't in control anymore. Fighting—that was my world. I understood that. I was *good* at it. In here, talking to her...that was the life I'd left behind when I'd retreated to my apartment.

Since that night I'd quit fighting, the closest I'd gotten to small talk was a few minutes of muttering in some woman's ear, just before I grabbed her hand and dragged her off to a cab so we could go to her place and have sex. Suddenly, I was back out here, talking to a woman, actually having a conversation, and it was jarring and weird and annoying as hell and...wonderful. It was bloody wonderful. I hated to admit it, but I was enjoying myself more than I had in a long time.

I looked at Sylvie across the table. She'd thrown on a loose t-shirt the same bright blue as the sky outside and her usual tight jeans. There wasn't anything inherently sexy about the t-shirt—it didn't even have a low neck. But every time she leaned forward or twisted, there was just a hint of the warm pressure of her breasts, pushing out the front of it. Even when her body was hidden, it was sexy as hell because then I could imagine it.

I am out of control with this woman.

"What about you?" I said gruffly, trying to get things back onto safer ground.

"Hotel maid," she said simply. "Picking up sheets and trash and sometimes dildos."

"Dil—"

"Don't worry, they give us gloves. You wouldn't believe some of the things people leave in their beds. The pay's shitty and the guests are always trying to get into your pants, but it's work." She finished her food and put down her fork. "I was in college, for a while. Dropped out when my dad died. Couldn't afford it."

I nodded sadly. Inside, though, what I felt was anger. Anger at fate for loading the dice when it came to her life. One crappy roll after another. No one did that to my angel. It wasn't fair. There were people who deserved that sort of luck, people like—

People like me?

I stood up. "I gotta go," I said. "I got a shift." I did, but it didn't start for another couple of hours. But I had to get out of there. For a second, while I was getting all righteously annoyed on her behalf, I'd thought of myself as one of the good guys. Like I could be the one to save her.

I could train her. Nothing more. The deeper I got into her life, the worse it would be for her. I wasn't any sort of good luck charm.

"What should we do about training?" she asked. "I'm kind of busy —I was thinking of taking on some extra shifts—"

I shook my head. "Don't. Cancel anything in the mornings."

"The *whole morning*? Every day?"

"You're in training, now."

"I need the money!"

"Money's no good to you if you're dead. Win the fight and you can pay the bills with your winnings."

She considered. "Okay," she said at last.

"Get some rest. Meet me at the docks, tomorrow. Wear running shoes. We gotta work on your stamina." I tossed some bills on the table to pay for lunch. "6:30."

I walked away before I got in any deeper. But I heard her call after me, "6:30 *am?*"

18

SYLVIE

G etting to the docks for 6:30am meant getting up not long after five. I couldn't remember when I'd last been awake at five, but I was pretty sure that it had involved staying up late, not getting up early.

When I reached the docks, I saw Aedan waiting for me outside the main gate. His face was upturned to the rising sun, as if he was bathing in pure morning. He hadn't seen me, yet, and he had an expression of beatific joy on his face, as if he was doing something he loved, something he hadn't done for a long time.

Which seemed weird. I mean, he was free and single. If he wanted to get up at this ungodly hour, he could, every morning. So why was he only doing it now?

Unless...he hadn't had a reason to, before.

"Hey," I said, to get his attention.

He looked around and, for just a second, I saw those big blue eyes shine as he looked at me. The way they lit up made my heart dance. A hot little thrill went through me, the sort I hadn't felt in a hell of a long time.

And then he seemed to catch himself and look away. I could

almost see his defenses slamming back up. His shoulders tightened, his brow furrowed. "You're late," he muttered.

It was 6:35. "There's no way you can possibly call this late. It's the middle of the night. We could go for a coffee and come back and it would *still* be too early." I yawned and considered that. "Actually, could we just do that?"

He ignored me and nodded at the road. "C'mon."

And he started to jog at an easy pace. Well, it was easy for the first hundred yards. Then I started to feel it.

"Okay," he said, not out of breath at all, "Now start punching. Jab, jab, jab, cross, like I showed you."

"While I'm running?"

"You think that girl you're fighting is going to stand still while you hit her?"

I tried to punch and run at the same time. It wasn't just doubly tiring, it was about ten times worse. Every punch threw off my stride. Every stagger threw off my punches.

"Come on," he told me. "Women are meant to be able to multi-task."

I huffed for air. "Traditionally," I managed, "aren't you meant to be riding a bike alongside me?"

"When you're running fast enough that I need a bike, I'll let you know."

We ran, with me *jab-jab-jab-cross*ing and him snapping orders at me. The sun slowly rose behind the cranes and moored ships, turning the water to glittering gold. I had to admit that I'd been missing out, never seeing sunrises.

We ran right down to the water, where there was an old, disused wooden pier. Some of it had collapsed and its stout wooden legs were all that were left on one side, stretching out into the water like stepping stones.

He veered off from me and jumped onto the first of the wooden legs, then jumped onto the next and the next, using them like stepping stones. When he reached the end, he turned on the spot and jumped back along them. He was as steady-footed as a mountain goat.

"I want you to try that, eventually," he said. "To work on your balance...and get you out of your head."

"Out of my *head?*"

"You're too much in your head. Not enough in your body." Was it just me, or had he hesitated before he'd said *body?* As if thinking of my body tripped him up. "You think too much. You need to feel it more."

I was still *jab-jab-jab-cross*ing, panting, now. "You've—lost—me," I managed.

He thought about how to explain it. He still wasn't out of breath. "Your body's just a vehicle, to you. Something to carry your brain. You've got to start feeling it. *Feel* the road under your feet. *Feel* each punch. Be in your body, not in your head."

It sounded like mystical boxer bullshit to me, but I nodded. And, as we ran on, I tried to do what he said. I tried to feel the air whistling past my fists as I punched. I tried to focus on the feel of my legs flexing with each step. I tried to stay out of my head and its thoughts of Aedan, jogging easily alongside me, his pecs stretching out his t-shirt, those wide shoulders rocking from side to side, his big blue eyes regarding me so solemnly....

"You're in your head again," he told me.

I gritted my teeth and kept trying. And slowly, despite the distraction of Aedan and his damn eyes, I started to feel it. It still sounded like mystical bullshit, but my body *did* start to feel more like *me* and less just a thing I gave orders to. I felt less floaty and distant, more grounded.

By the time we reached the halfway point and turned back the way we'd come, it felt natural. By the time we reached the pier again, I was buzzing with the feeling. My muscles ached and my lungs burned, but I felt alive.

I veered off the street and ran for the pier. It was still too early for traffic and it was so quiet that I could hear every scrape of my shoes on the asphalt, every rasp of the fabric of my sports top as I twisted and punched. As I approached the stepping-stone pier legs, I quit punching and held my arms out for balance.

"Um—" said Aedan.

I ignored him. How hard could it be? I jumped to the first one...and landed, swaying a little. *Shit.* The legs weren't as big as they'd looked, maybe a foot in diameter. But I couldn't stop now. I jumped again and landed on the next one, swaying a little more. Another. Another. I was over the water, now, and it suddenly looked a long way down—eight or ten feet.

"Sylvie, I said you should try it *eventually....*" Aedan called from behind me.

In less than thirty days, I was going to be in The Pit. I couldn't afford *eventually.*

I jumped again. One foot hit the pier leg...but right at the edge, and the other foot missed it completely. My stomach lurched as I felt myself tip to one side, arms windmilling...and then I was falling towards the water.

19

AEDAN

I watched in horror as she hit the surface almost headfirst. She hadn't had time to get her arms out so she plunged right under, going down deep.

I raced to the edge and dived in. The water was colder than it had any right to be in the summer, and it wasn't the cleanest, either. But I could see her beneath me, her long hair fanning out around her like a dark halo. I grabbed her under the arms and hauled her up.

We broke the surface together, gasping in air and daylight. She spluttered a little, but seemed okay.

"You gotta work up to it," I panted, "you daft mare."

She tossed her wet hair out of her face, sending gleaming jewels of water out in arcs. Then she looked at me. "Sorry."

"I'll take you to my place to dry off. It's not far."

We swam and then waded ashore. It was worse, once we were out. Our clothes seemed to have absorbed half the water in the harbor and our shoes squelched. Neither of us felt like running anymore, so we trudged back along the street leaving a trail of water behind us.

For a while, we walked in silence. Then a sudden splatter of water made me glance to the side. Sylvie had twisted her long hair into a rope and was wringing it out, arching her back so the water missed her back as it fell. That meant her chest was thrust out, and—

Her running top and bra were plastered to her breasts and the water had chilled her enough that her nipples were standing out hard through the fabric. I lost all capacity for rational thought for a few seconds.

She realized I was staring at her. "What?" she asked, bemused.

"...nothing."

I forced my eyes forward and told myself I would not—absolutely *would not*—look at her again. I'd keep my eyes off her all the way to my place like a feckin' gentleman.

Except when we reached a side road and I had to look both ways.

And when I thought I might be walking too fast, or too slow.

And sometimes when I needed to just, you know, check she was okay.

This woman had stripped all my self control away in just a few hours.

"You live here?" she asked when we arrived at my apartment building. She was careful to make it sound neutral, but I knew what she meant. Suddenly, she understood why I was okay for money. I just nodded.

As soon as I opened the door, I wished I'd cleaned up. I'm not a slob, but...well, guys have different priorities, when it comes to cleaning. I kicked some pizza boxes under a table.

To my surprise, she went straight over to the shelf over the TV. I'd gotten so used to the trophies being there, they didn't even register.

"You won all these?" she asked in wonder.

I shrugged.

"*County* Champion?"

"Only in my weight category. And it was years ago."

She picked up another one. "*Twice?*" She spun to face me. "What the hell were you doing fighting in The Pit? Why aren't you on the pro circuit?"

I shook my head. "A lot of stuff happened, back in Ireland. When I came over here, things were a little...complicated."

"To do with your family?"

I stared at her. "Didn't you want to get out of those clothes? I'll find you something to wear."

She stared back at me stubbornly for a moment but, when it became obvious I wasn't going to break, she headed for the bathroom.

I let out a long breath and tidied a few more things away. Then I stripped out of my clothes, toweled off and pulled on clean pants and a t-shirt. And then I stopped, because I was listening.

I could hear her undressing.

Never in my life had I imagined that just the sound of clothes hitting the ground could be so sexy. But that heavy thump could only be her soaked sweatpants. That wet stretching, peeling sound must be her running top coming off. A creak of elastic—her bra coming off. And now she'd be standing there topless, her breasts dripping wet, nipples hard from the cold. Right there, not six feet away from me, on the other side of a thin wooden door.

The sound of wet fabric rubbing past skin. Her panties. I heard the sodden cotton hit the tiles and then she was completely nude. In my mind, I could see her naked ass shining with little beads of water, and between her thighs...what? Was she shaved? Waxed? I wanted to see her lips. Kiss them. Lick them.

The door opened and her head stuck out. "Um...you were going to find me something to wear?"

I dug in my closet and found a t-shirt and a pair of shorts. Then I had to hand them to her. Which meant walking right up to that damp, suspicious face and trying to forget that it was attached to a damp and very naked body.

She could have stretched her arm out, so that I didn't have to come so close. But she kept it right up against the door, so I had to come close. Really close. Until our faces were only a foot apart.

Come to think of it, why hadn't I stretched *my* arm out to pass the clothes to her?

Too late now.

I put the clothes into her hand, but for some reason I didn't let go of them.

"Thank you," she said, and pulled the clothes a half-inch towards her.

I still didn't let go.

She looked up into my eyes. I saw her go through a whole range of different emotions, lightning fast. Surprise. Doubt. Her eyes went big and she took a little breath in. *Lust.*

Does she want this to happen? I sure did. At this point, my cock was ready to break its way through the feckin' door. One kiss. I'd still be snogging her when I lifted her naked body in my arms and carried her to the bed.

No. Jesus, Aedan, stop thinking with your cock. That was okay with the women I picked up in bars. We both knew what we were getting into, then. Sylvie would expect more than a one-night stand. She deserved more. And I couldn't give it to her.

I let go of the clothes.

She frowned, confused...and then it turned to anger. She ducked back into the bathroom and slammed the door.

She put on the fresh clothes faster than I would have thought possible. When she came out, the t-shirt hanging almost to her knees and the shorts in severe danger of falling down, it should have been funny. It would have been, if it hadn't been for her expression. "Do you have a bag?" she snapped.

I found a plastic grocery bag and passed it to her. She went back into the bathroom and started squeezing the water out of her wet clothes. The door was open and I watched as she twisted her sweatpants into a rope. It looked a lot like she was wringing someone's neck. Then she shook them out, as loudly and violently as possible. Every time she moved, the shorts threatened to fall down and she had to stop and grab at them, and that only seemed to make her madder.

Maybe I messed that up.

"I'll see you tomorrow," she said stiffly. "At the gym. Okay? Eight?" She crammed her clothes into the bag so hard it nearly ripped.

I definitely messed that up. "Um. Yeah. Eight."

She stalked out of the bathroom and over to the door. I spoke up just as she turned the handle. "Sylvie?"

She looked over her shoulder, eyebrows raised. I felt myself falling into those gorgeous, liquid eyes. *Say something, you idiot! Make it right! Tell her—*

What? That I really liked her? That I wanted more than just sex? That I'd never met anyone like her before?

"Will you be okay, walking in wet shoes?" I asked.

"Yeah," she said. "Yeah, I'll be just fucking fine walking in wet fucking shoes."

And she slammed the door.

There are some times when banging your head against a wall isn't sufficient. As soon as my shift was done, I resolved to get very, very drunk instead. Drunk enough that I could forget all about Sylvie and her wet running top and her unseen, naked breasts in my bathroom. Drunk enough that I could resolve to stop all this, all the little moments and glances and nearly-kisses. Stop them before they drove us both crazy. Before she got close enough to see me for what I really was and fled, leaving her without any preparation at all for the fight.

From now on, it had to be all business.

20

SYLVIE

Why didn't he kiss me?

I'd asked myself the same question several hundred different ways, but I wasn't any closer to an answer. For days, I'd been sure that he liked me. I'd been one hundred percent sure that he'd been about to kiss me, when I'd been poking my head out of the bathroom. And then, just as everything should have come together, he'd backed off.

I told myself that it didn't matter. That I'd just focus on what mattered—the fight. I told myself that it had been stupid of me to act like some lovesick teenager when things were so serious.

But it wasn't as simple as that. As soon as I stopped thinking about him in that way, I realized what I was missing. My feelings for him had been the only thing holding back the fear of what was going to happen in less than a month. Without that one positive thing in my life, the fear took over.

Besides, it wasn't just about me. I knew something was wrong. I knew he was hurting inside because of something in his past. I owed him. Every day, he was helping me—saving me. And there wasn't a damn thing I could do to help him, if he wouldn't open up and let me in.

I had no choice. I locked my feelings down tight, and only let them creep out when I was on my own in the apartment, in my bed, my fingers stealing down between my thighs and under my panties. And when I visited Alec in hospital, I'd perch on the edge of his bed, put my head close to his and whisper in his ear about the gorgeous man I couldn't have.

And we trained.

We trained for two weeks, five hours a day, six days a week. I'd never worked so hard in my life. Every day started with a run and then a long session in the gym, with just a quick break for lunch. In the afternoons, Aedan would go to the docks to work while I'd retreat to my apartment and sleep, curled up like a cat on top of the covers. It was my only chance to catch up on rest before my evening shift at the hotel. I'd cancelled my morning shifts to train so the evening shifts were vital to keep some money coming in. Without Alec's income, the bills were piling up rapidly. Aedan was right, though: the money wouldn't be any use to me if I was dead. Winning the fight was everything.

He worked on my core with endless rounds of crunches and medicine ball twists. He built up my strength by getting me to pump iron, whispering encouragement in my ear when my arms trembled and I thought I was going to drop the weight on myself. He got me to hit punch bags, pads and, eventually, him.

My body started to change—and fast. It wasn't magic; it was the sheer brute force of the training. My midsection lost its pudginess and became taut and toned. My arms started to develop shape. My legs became leaner, from the endless squats and footwork.

I wasn't ready for a fight, yet, but Aedan had me try light sparring, both of us in gloves and head protectors. He let me go at him again and again: he fended off my attacks with casual ease, but that wasn't the point. The point was to find my style.

"You're an out-boxer," he told me. "Fast. Good on your feet. You hit from a distance. You don't have much power, but you can wear the other girl down, wait until she makes a mistake."

I thought about that for a second. I quite liked the idea of not having to get too close. Hopefully, that meant I'd get hit less. "What are you?"

"A brawler." He smiled. He did that more often, these days, and when he did all that darkness just dropped away. "Slow and stupid. I just hit them—hard." He crossed his arms and regarded me. "It's like rock-paper-scissors. Each style's got an advantage over another, and each one's beaten by another."

"So who do I have to watch out for?"

"A swarmer. They'll get right up in your face and hit you with flurries of punches—they'll overwhelm you. A swarmer'll be beaten by a brawler, like me."

"And who do *you* have to watch out for?"

"You."

I blinked at him.

"Out-boxers can beat brawlers. I'm only dangerous if I can get in close—like this." He stepped right up close, so close that I had to look up to look into his eyes. He took my hand in both of his and used it tap himself on the jaw, pushing himself back. "So what you need to do is keep me at arm's length. Where I can't hurt you." He was still holding my wrist, his fingers hot on my skin. I felt his hand tighten.

"Understand?" he asked, his voice strained.

I nodded.

He let out a long, slow breath and we went back to it.

And I focused on keeping him at a distance.

I didn't think I'd ever get used to the huge, high-protein boxer's breakfasts. But after a week, I could shovel down my steak and eggs and be hungry for chicken and vegetables a few hours later. My weight went up, but the mirror showed I was leaner. The fat was burning off and being replaced by muscle.

Each morning, Aedan would have me shadow box so that I could see how I looked to someone else. At first, it was comical: my tiny, weak shadow throwing punches while his muscular bulk stood watching next to it. But after a few weeks, I began to see changes. I moved faster. I was leaner...*meaner.*

It still didn't feel right, though—hitting something. It didn't feel natural, in the way I suspected it felt natural to Aedan. Maybe it comes naturally to men.

During one of the long bag sessions—I don't know how many punches I'd thrown, but it felt like *infinity plus three*—I mumbled something about this to Aedan. Who shook his head.

"You think you're weak because you're a woman," he told me. "You're not."

"We *are*. Physically, we are."

"Not mentally, though, and that's what it's all about." He looked at me seriously. "What you did, volunteering to take Alec's place...you *are* strong, Sylvie. Stronger than anyone I've ever met."

I gave him a look, my cheeks flushing, and hit the bag again.

He grabbed my elbows and held my arms back so I couldn't punch again. "Say it with me," he ordered. "*I am strong.*"

"I am strong," I mumbled, embarrassed.

"Like you mean it."

I twisted around to look at him. I was all ready to say something snarky but something in his expression stopped me. I'd never seen him looking so solemn, so....

Jesus, he almost looked *impressed* with me.

I looked back at the bag. "I am strong," I said. It didn't sound so stupid, this time.

"Again."

"I am strong."

He let my arms go and I hit the bag as hard as I could.

～

Keeping my mind on the training wasn't easy with Aedan around. I knew he was trying to keep things professional and I was, too. But that didn't stop things happening—little moments that would stay with me the rest of the day. Like he'd pass me the water bottle to drink out of and it would still be warm from his touch. Or he'd really lay into the punch bag to show me a technique and emerge all sweaty and perfect, his shoulders gleaming, and I'd have to drag my eyes off of him.

The training was working—I could feel it. But every day, the attraction between us was growing tighter, pulling us together. Little things. Like we'd walk to the diner, and we'd walk closer together. Closer than trainer and pupil should walk. I told myself that it was just because we were friends. Or we'd share a joke, despite—or maybe because—of how serious things were. We'd blow off steam by doing something stupid, like emptying a water bottle over the other one's head and...I found myself laughing more easily and more genuinely than I ever had. And *he* was definitely smiling more...but each time, he'd catch himself and get serious again, pushing me away.

Once, on a really scorching day, the air conditioning in the gym went on the fritz and the place became unbearable. Aedan took me out into the disused lot behind the building and had me hit pads in the open air, with the sun beating down on us. After a half hour, he stripped off his tank top and I saw him topless for the first time. Jesus. I'd known he was in good shape, but he was *ripped.* His pecs looked like they were carved from stone. His abs had deliciously hard ridges on them that I immediately wanted to run my fingers over and there was a centerline running all the way up, from just where I'd kiss the base of his neck, to just where I'd finish kissing his top half, before I proceeded down below....

Ahem.

It was only when he turned around that I spotted the tattoo. He only had one, a small shamrock right in the middle of his upper back, over his spine—it must have been painful as hell to get.

"Ireland?" I asked when I saw it.

He turned around to face me, looking a little surprised that I'd noticed it. Did he not know I was drinking in every inch of his body? "Brotherhood," he said at last.

Things came to a head near the end of the second week. I was standing with him in the ring when I realized I'd left my gloves down on the floor. I bent over the ropes to get them, bending almost double with my ass high in the air and my hands down near my feet.

When I turned around, Aedan was standing there watching me. It hit me that he'd been staring right at my ass, upthrust and presented to him. And when I happened to glance down, I could see it—a long, thick bulge along his thigh, standing out through the thin material of his shorts. Jesus, he was big. And hard. For me.

When I finally got my gloves on, my fists kept slipping off the bag because I couldn't get the image of his hard-on out of my mind. It soaked down through me again and again, lighting me up and pooling as liquid heat at my groin.

That night, I ran a hot bath to soak the aches away. I lay there and soaped everywhere, studiously avoiding the area below my waist and above my knees. I wasn't even going to get close. I wasn't going to tempt myself. I was absolutely *not* going to start jilling off to memories of Aedan and the bulge in his pants and how he'd been watching me, bent over the ropes, and what might have happened if the gym had been empty and he'd suddenly stepped up behind me and ripped my sweatpants down my thighs and pushed my legs apart and oh God—

I came, back arched, hips jerking, foam and water splashing. When I finished, I lay there, sated but guilty. *He* was managing to keep things under control. Why couldn't I?

21

AEDAN

We trained for two weeks solid.

Sylvie was working her ass off, slamming the bag and really improving her footwork. In fact, I was starting to see that she had real potential—fate had thrown me a bone. This scared, sweet angel, who'd never hit anything her entire life, had the agility and speed to really go places. In some other life, if she'd started young and been paired with a proper trainer instead of a dumb fighter like me, maybe she would have wound up doing women's boxing professionally. Here and now, though, I just had to pray that her potential and my experience were enough to see her through this one fight.

And me?

I watched Sylvie.

I heard myself speaking, saying things like, "Keep your hands up," and "Watch your balance." But the training was almost automatic, happening in some far off part of my brain, because every last scrap of my conscious mind was filled with *her*.

Her hair, long dark strands of it whipping around as she ducked and weaved.

Her breasts: soft, perfect mounds I couldn't drag my eyes from.

When she was hitting the speedball and they were bouncing in their sports bra, it was bloody hypnotic.

Her smile, not easily given but a glorious prize every time I won it.

I was becoming obsessed and I knew it.

I had two more weeks to get Sylvie ready for her fight and I honestly didn't know if I could control myself that long. Every day was worse. Every day we got cruelly closer, while knowing we couldn't take the final step. It was torture.

Every time I hit a bag or a pad to demonstrate something, it was like a drug had been released into my system. Using my fists again felt so good I wanted to weep. Every impact was a reminder of what I really was: a monster.

And then came the day I'd been dreading. The day I had to hit her.

22

SYLVIE

"Fight?" I asked nervously.

"Gotta do it eventually," said Aedan. He sounded as reluctant as I did. Why? It wasn't like I had any chance of hurting *him*. "It's like driving a car. You can practice the pedals and changing gears as much as you like, but eventually you've gotta get on the road."

Up until now, we'd only tried very light sparring with me pulling my punches, or he'd come at me gently and I'd tried to block. Not actual *fighting*. I swallowed and looked up at him, scared, as he slipped a helmet on me. It was oddly claustrophobic, even though my whole face was exposed. I couldn't hear properly. My head felt heavy. "I'm not sure about this," I said.

He nodded somberly and pulled on his gloves. In the real fight, of course, I'd be bare knuckle. But I couldn't train like that without messing up my hands, so gloves it was. I still hadn't mastered getting the second glove on so I did what I always did and used my teeth to pull its strap into tight. I caught him looking at me. "What?" I mumbled, the strap clamped between my teeth.

He shook his head as if to say, *nothing.*

We squared up to one another. "We'll go for three minutes," he said, looking at the clock. "Just like the real thing. Remember: *keep me away,* okay? That's where your advantage is—at arm's length."

I nodded.

And it began.

He let me warm up a little to start with, letting me circle him and get into my rhythm. Fighting, I was learning, was a lot like dancing. It's okay as long as you're in the flow, but once you lose it, you've lost it and it's hard to get it back again. As the seconds ticked by, I felt myself loosening up, darting in and out of range. I was starting to really see the differences between us. He was all solid, hard power, his powerful shoulders and biceps hinting at the damage he'd do if I dared to get within range of him. I was faster than him—there was just no way he could dance around like I could. But I didn't wield anything like the same power. My only hope was to whittle him down slowly. It was like being a bee, buzzing around a grunting, pawing bull. I had to land a hundred good hits; he only had to land one.

But I couldn't hit him.

Not even once.

It wasn't like hitting the bag, or hitting pads, or even the times we'd sparred and he'd told me to try to tap one of his gloves, or his side, or the side of his head. This was me, actually trying to land a punch on him.

"Come on," he grunted. "Come at me."

I shuffled closer. Backed off. Shuffled closer again. I could feel my heart racing. *Hit him?!* I didn't want to hit him. He was...*Aedan.* There wasn't anyone I wanted to hit less.

"Forget it's me," he told me sharply, as if reading my mind. "Pretend it's someone else, if you have to." His jaw tightened. "Make me some guy who's hurt you."

My mind went back to The Pit. The scrape of the concrete wall against my naked ass. That bastard's hand, cupping my sex.

I flew at him, aiming hooks at his kidneys. He blocked one and deflected the other, but had to step back a little, lowering his guard. I knew what I had to do next—go for the face. I launched a jab at that gorgeous, hard jaw—

And my fist skirted wide. I couldn't do it. I couldn't hit him and I couldn't pretend he was someone else. Not when I felt like this about him.

His mouth drew back into a snarl. "Come on!"

I went for the head again, but my hits were half-hearted. Hitting him was like trying to injure myself—my brain just refused to do it.

"You better come at me," he grunted. "Because I'm going to come at you."

And then he did.

23

AEDAN

it her.

I'd known what I had to do ever since I'd climbed into the ring. Hell, I'd known it the moment she'd come to me on the docks. But that didn't mean I could do it. Moments ago, I'd been staring at her as she tried to use her teeth to do up her glove, so feckin' cute I wanted to weep. Now I had to hit her?!

She probably thought I was taking it easy on her, letting her warm up. The truth was, I couldn't lay into her. I waited for her to hit me, hoping that once the fight got going, it would be easier to open up on her. But she didn't want to hit me either—I could see it in her eyes. I tried to goad her into it, even tried to get her to think of me as some guy who'd hurt her, which made my guts twist. But any anger I roused in her was gone in a second. She couldn't follow through.

And that meant it was time to hit her.

I waded into it, knocking aside her punches and getting closer, pushing her back towards the ropes. She blocked the first two jabs I threw at her but the third one sent her off balance. She staggered back, her guard down.

Now. I had to show her what happened when she dropped her guard. If she never got hit, she'd never get over her fear.

I raised my fist. My guts knotted. Jesus, she looked so beautiful, so soft and delicate. *How do guys do this? Why would anyone want to break something this amazing?*

I had to.

I hit her with one good blow to the side of the head, making sure it landed on the padded helmet. Maybe half my usual power. She staggered sideways and I saw the flash of shock in her eyes. *Feck.*

I was back to being a monster again. Or maybe I'd never stopped.

But it had worked. She'd had that first hit—I'd popped her cherry and now she knew it wasn't going to kill her. She came at me again, pushing me back with a good combo. I relaxed a little and got in a quick little hook, signaling it well so that she'd be able to block it.

But her eyes were on mine. Distracted, she lifted her arms out of the way...just as my fist swung into her side. I felt the hardness of ribs against my glove...and she went down.

24

SYLVIE

Pain exploded in my side, red-hot fire that turned to numbing cold. My whole left side seemed to go weak. Just being upright was too painful, so my legs crumpled under me and dumped me to the mat. The shock of hitting it started the pain all over again.

My head bounced off the mat, that sudden, shocking slam, like being a kid again and slipping on the bouncy castle. If it had been the concrete floor of The Pit, my skull would have cracked open.

The bright lights above me were blocked out by Aedan. He came down on one knee beside me, his face contorted with horror.

He's down on one knee, thrilled some far-off part of my brain.

"*Are you okay?*" he yelled.

I frowned. What did those words mean? I wondered if maybe I'd hit my head. I thought I remembered something like that happening.

Buttercups.

"*Are you okay?*" he yelled again. And then his voice seemed to become clearer and the lights didn't seem quite so bright and I stopped thinking about buttercups and—

I blinked at him and nodded. *Christ,* my side hurt.

He ripped off his gloves. Then his hand was sliding up under my t-shirt, feeling my ribs. There was the pounding ache of a bruise, but I didn't feel the sharp pain that would mean broken bones. His hand moved higher, probing gently.

I locked eyes with him. I was lying very still, getting used to the feeling of the rubbery mat under my back. I knew moving would hurt.

His hand reached the top of my ribcage and he stopped there. He let out a sort of pant of exasperation. "You were meant to block that, you feckin' idiot!" But his eyes didn't say *angry*. His eyes were terrified...and relieved.

"Sorry," I whispered.

We stared at one another. He was looking at me the way a mother looks at the child she's just dragged out of the path of a truck. Then, as the seconds passed, the fear and relief died away. And....

Both of us seemed to become aware of where his hand was at the same time. His palm was under my t-shirt, right at the top of my ribcage. The edge of his hand was pushed up against the underside of my breast, lifting it a little. The heat of him throbbed into me.

And then suddenly his other hand was cupping my cheek, the tips of his fingers in my hair, and his mouth was coming down on mine.

25

SYLVIE

It happened so fast that I only just had time to close my eyes. A firework went off in my brain, its explosions spelling out *YES!*

His lips were hard and hot, capturing mine and pushing them wide, demanding I open. I've never experienced such a moment of going weak as when those lips hit mine. It was as if two week's worth of pent-up male frustration poured into me. All those times he'd looked at me. All those times one of us had pushed the other away.

I opened, feeling weirdly perfumed and soft under his aggression. Yet when his tongue touched me, it didn't plunge in. His lips held mine braced open, my mouth vulnerable, while the tip of his tongue just licked around the very inside of my lips, every hot contact sending a scorching shudder through my body. I writhed under him, the throbbing in my side melting into insignificance as the pleasure soaked down through me. His knee was between my legs and—God, I could feel the hot, hard tip of him pressing against my thigh through our clothes. Throbbing. Ready.

His tongue finally met mine, dancing with it, both of us panting together as things slid inexorably in one direction. His hand brushed down my ribs, going lightly over the place it hurt, barely brushing my skin. Then it returned, this time pushing harder when it reached my breast. My whole body went tense. Would he—

His hand slid smoothly up over the soft flesh with no hesitation. His hand captured my breast and gently squeezed and, even through the thickness of the sports bra, it felt amazing. Where his thumb rubbed across the naked skin, it felt as if it left a burning trail. I immediately wanted his hands all over me, both of us naked, our bodies rubbing together until every damn inch of me had felt him.

I moaned up into his mouth, my tongue fighting with his, desperate to sample him. He was hardness and brute strength and salty, raw power.

He reluctantly broke the kiss, leaving two last panting kisses on my lower lip, and said. "Let's go somewhere else." And then he was lifting me up to my feet and then, almost immediately, heaving me up over the ropes and down to the floor, swinging me through the air like a doll. He jumped down beside me and pulled off our helmets, then stripped off our gloves. He grabbed my hand and towed me towards the locker room.

The *men's* locker room.

Just as we got to the door, he pushed me up against the wall and said, "Wait." He kissed me again and it pinned me there as securely as a butterfly speared with a pin.

I felt him leave me and duck into the locker room. I kept my eyes closed. There was the sound of coins going into a machine and then the metal clank as it dispensed something. Then he was back, grabbing my hand again and towing me along.

When I opened my eyes, I glimpsed the condom in his other hand. A deep, hot throb went through me.

He pushed through a door and led me down a hallway I'd never been in. There was a stairwell at the end with a *No Admittance* sign hanging on a chain across it.

He stepped right over it, and lifted me over as well. Then we were climbing the stairs. Halfway up, he started kissing me again and we stumbled up like that, blindly feeling for the handrail. At the top, we pushed through another door, eyes still closed. I felt the sudden warmth of sun on my skin....

I opened my eyes and saw that we were on top of the building, the city spread out around us. A low wall around the edge would provide some privacy...if we lay down.

My stomach flipped over and then exploded into deep, dark heat. *Jesus, are we really going to do this? Now? I could be dead in a few weeks!*

And part of me answered, *that's exactly why we should.* I needed to feel alive. I wanted this more than ever.

He pushed me up against an air conditioning duct, the metal sun-warm through my top. He raked his fingers through my hair. "Christ," he muttered, "Christ, I've wanted you. Since I saw you in that fecking dump of a place."

I remembered him looking at me, back at The Pit. "Then why didn't you—"

He gritted his teeth and shook his head. "You shouldn't get involved with me."

"Why?"

"I'm...bad, Sylvie. I've done bad shit."

"I don't care." And I realized I didn't.

"You should."

"Well, I don't. I don't care what you did in the past."

He grimaced. I could see him tensing up, battling with himself. Any second, he was going to tear away from me and stomp away down the stairs and I might lose him forever. That was unthinkable. I grabbed his head in my hands and, this time, *I* kissed *him*, showing him how much I needed him.

He growled. "This is a bad idea."

"No, no, it's a good idea," I babbled.

He stared into my eyes. The wind whipped my hair into my eyes and he brushed it away, letting the strands slide through his fingers.

"Ah, the hell with it," he said. And kissed me full-on and completely, his whole body flattening mine against the air conditioning duct. I gave a low moan of relief. My hands came up and felt for him, grabbing at his sides through the soft cotton of his tank top. God, he felt like oak underneath. My hands had been tingling for weeks at the imagined sensation of him under my palms. Now it was real, the hard ridges of his ribs and then, sliding around, the firm muscles of his back.

His hands were under my t-shirt, lifting it up. I felt the tickle of wind and sun on my exposed sides and then the cloth was peeling up over my sports bra, off my arms...off completely. We had to break the kiss as it slid over my head and I opened my eyes, staring up at him. He held my gaze for a second...and then he looked down over my body, eating up the sight of me. The raw hunger in his eyes made me squirm, the feeling twisting down and turning to warm slickness between my thighs.

His hands stroked outwards across my stomach. Every individual cell in my skin seemed to come alive, tingling and crackling. I arched my back away from the duct, pushing myself into his hands. The pain in my side came back as I moved, but the pleasure sluiced it away. His hands slid higher and higher, moving towards my breasts.

"Wait," he muttered. He tore himself away from me and stepped back, but only half a step. "I'm nothin' if not a gentleman," he said breathlessly. "I have to check you're not concussed. You seeing double?"

There was only one gorgeous, muscled Irishman in front of me. "No," I panted.

"Follow my finger." He moved it back and forth in front of my eyes. I tracked it, resisting the urge to grab it and shove it into my mouth.

"What day is it?" he panted.

"Thursday!"

"Friday." He shrugged. "Feck it. Close enough." And he was grabbing my head between his hands again, cupping my cheeks as he kissed me. His hands were on my hips, spinning us around so that I came away from the air conditioning duct, and his hands were sliding up under my sports bra, hooking it off, peeling the fabric away from my body. My breasts lifted and then bounced free, the shock of the outdoor air on them making me gasp. He pulled my bra off and tossed it away.

I opened my eyes to see him gazing down at my breasts, his eyes heavy-lidded with lust. "Christ," he said. "You've got the best tits this side of the Atlantic, girl. Feckin' perfect." He filled his hands with them, lifting and then squeezing with just the right amount of pressure, and I groaned. Then his thumbs started to stroke across my nipples, making them rise and harden with soft, expert swirls. I felt my hips begin to grind and thrash, trying to get friction on my sex. It was everything I could do to resist shoving my hand straight down there to rub myself. But my hands were busy exploring his back, roaming over the thick muscles of his shoulders, delighting at the way the landscape bunched and changed every time he moved.

I grabbed the hem of his tank top and pulled it up, peeling it off his muscled core and then over the wide swell of his pecs. He reluctantly let go of my breasts for a moment while it came up and over his head, then recaptured them. I slid my hands around to his front, feeling the shape of his chest, caressing the pecs and stroking my thumbs over his pink, dime-sized nipples until he growled.

He suddenly ducked down, breaking free of my hands, and I gasped as his mouth found my breast. The sun had been warm on my skin, but his lips and tongue were blazing hot. His tongue flicked over my nipple, fast and savage, then licked the smooth flesh again and again. My fingers knitted into his hair, clutching him there, never wanting to let him go.

He opened his mouth wider and engulfed as much of my breast as he could fit in, sucking me in, playing his tongue over the softness and then lashing over the nipple. I squeezed my eyes tight shut, rocked on my heels and pressed myself hard against his mouth. His hand grabbed at my other breast, squeezing and fondling, working at it with just a little roughness. Letting me know what it would be like when we got to the sex—hard and fast and unrelenting. The twisting heat inside me spun even faster.

He released my breast and I felt the sun beating down on the spit-slick skin. His hand played over it one last time, as if he couldn't bear to let it go, and the feel of his rough thumb drawn slowly over my wet nipple nearly made me explode.

He kissed his way slowly down my stomach, each kiss feather-light and scalding hot. The sun was hot on our skin and, when I opened my eyes, it was glaringly bright. But I felt as if I was heating up from the inside, the need at my core making me glow as if I was made of hot coals, and every touch made me burn hotter. When he reached the waistband of my sweatpants, he looked up at me. It wasn't so much a *Do you want me to?* It was more an *I'm going to: grab hold of something.*

I dug my fingers into the hair at the back of his head and braced myself.

He didn't pull my sweatpants down, as I expected. He hooked his thumbs under the waistband and folded it back on itself, baring just an inch of skin all the way around my body. That put the top of my panties on show. He kissed along the top of them, following the line from hip to hip. Then he folded back another inch, sweatpants and panties together.

I was staring down at myself and my breath caught in my throat as I saw myself bared. There was something very intense about seeing myself revealed bit by bit, and seeing him staring at me as it happened. We could see the paler skin of my pubis, now. He licked it, drawing his tongue up it in little flicks, and I growled and ground my hips.

He folded back another inch of fabric, the action more of a roll, now, and this time he revealed hair, as black as the hair on my head and gleaming in the fierce sunlight. For the first time, I glanced around. We were the tallest building for a few streets around and the wall at the edge probably shielded us from anyone on the ground, but if someone in a high-rise had binoculars....

He started kissing me through the soft curls of hair, probing through it with his tongue, touching the sensitive skin beneath. I heard him inhale the scent of me, his lungs filling, and there was something primal, almost animal about it. The sight of him crouched in front of me, his body hugely powerful compared to mine, made my head swim.

He rolled the fabric down again, the elastic tight around the middle of my ass cheeks. My breath came quicker—God, he could see me...see *everything*. I'd never been exposed like this before, outside in the bright sunlight. I almost said something—we could lie down, at least, and hide behind the wall a little. But then I felt his breath against my clit and I stiffened. His tongue flicked out, teasing the little bud, and I gasped.

Another few inches of fabric and I was bared completely, the wadded-up waistband now just under my ass cheeks. He pushed his head between my thighs, his upper lip toying with my clit, his tongue licking underneath to run the full length of my lips. I gave a little shriek and opened my legs as far as my bunched-up clothes would allow, which was only a few inches.

His mouth pressed closer. The tip of his tongue ran back and forth along the line where my lips met and I felt myself opening for him. He teased and teased and then suddenly plunged inside, with a movement that seemed to come from his whole upper body. I groaned as he slid on my inner flesh. I couldn't believe how wet I was already.

He began to thrust with his tongue, pumping at me. At the same time, his hands grabbed my ass cheeks and began to squeeze in rhythm. I felt myself carried along by it, bucking my hips against him to the same slow beat. He angled his head, going deeper, his tongue pushing and twisting inside me. I folded at the waist, wrapping myself around him; I wanted to collapse on top of him, it felt so great. I could feel the flat of his tongue opening me up, preparing me for...I thought of the outline of his cock through his shorts. For *that*. Big and thick and long and pushing up—

I clutched at his head even harder. I wanted this, but I wanted him—*needed* him inside me. "Aedan," I moaned. "God, Aedan...."

He started to pump his tongue faster, his upper lip rubbing back and forth over my clit, soft and smooth against the engorged little nub. I realized he had no intention of stopping. *He's going to do it. He's going to do it and I'm going to come, right here, on top of a goddamn building, and there's nothing I can do about it—*

He reached up with one hand and squeezed my breast again. Then he took the nipple between finger and thumb, gently drawing them along its length, and I went wild. I felt the heat twist and pull tight inside me, the pressure building and building. His tongue thrust and his lip crushed against my clit, the hardness of his mouth rolling against it, and then pinched my nipple just a little—

My fingers dug so hard into his scalp that it must have hurt. The pleasure throbbed through me in long, hot waves, making me writhe and flex. I pulled him hard against me, grinding my sex against his mouth, feeling my juices sticky against his lips. My throat hurt and I realized I was yelling something.

I slowly released him and he leaned back so that he could look up at me. There was a truly wicked grin on his face and probably a helpless, goofy one on mine.

He stood up, wrapped his arms around me, and picked me up. My breasts squashed against his naked chest and I groaned at how good it felt, how every little contact of his muscles against my nipples made me tremble. He kissed me long and deep, and I could taste myself on his lips. His hands played up and down my back and then down to my naked ass, cupping me there, handling my weight easily.

He walked me over to a clear patch of rooftop. Every step made my hardened nipples scrape against his chest, reducing me to a hot, panting mess all over again. When he finally stopped and crouched down to put me down, my mind was taffy.

My naked ass touched the sun-warm concrete first, then he rolled me gently down until my whole upper body was down and my legs were in the air. He pulled off my sneakers and pulled my bunched-up sweatpants and panties off my legs, leaving me naked. My feet flopped down, my knees bent and slightly spread, and we stared at each other. He knelt beside me, topless but otherwise decent, and I lay there naked and wanton, my body still flushed from my orgasm. I could feel his eyes roving over every inch of me and that just made me hotter.

When his gaze finally reached my face, those big blue Irish eyes were burning like fire. Keeping them locked on me, he knelt up. He pushed his pants and shorts down his legs and his cock sprang out, already rock hard.

I gulped. It was even bigger than it had looked through his clothes, with a satiny head and a thick, long shaft. The shadow of it fell across my stomach and I squirmed inside.

He stared at me, his eyes raking down the length of my body a few times and then back to my eyes. And he began to stroke himself.

I'd never had that—never had a man stroke himself at the sight of me. I wasn't ready for what a turn on it was. There was something so completely filthy about it, especially with it happening out in the open air, with the sun warming our bodies and the breeze licking over us.

Without thinking, I slid a hand down my body and between my thighs. And I started to play my fingertips up and down over my slickened lips, watching him watching me. Staring at those ridged abs and powerful thighs. Thinking about how they'd power that thick cock into me.

We stayed there, wordlessly touching ourselves, for long minutes, the speed building slowly, until we couldn't take it anymore. He suddenly launched himself forward with a growl and kissed me, pushing my head back against the concrete, my hair cushioning me as he ravished my mouth.

"Enough," he told me. He rolled on the condom. "I need to fuck you."

He pushed between my thighs and I opened them, feeling the dusty scrape of the roof under my bare feet. Then the thick head of his cock was toying with my folds. "Christ, Sylvie," he muttered, staring down at me. "I've wanted this for so long. You're fecking beautiful, girl."

A deep, hot bomb went off in my chest. I reached up for him with both arms. "Do it," I said breathlessly.

The tip of him parted me and then he was pushing, entering me easily. God, I don't think I've ever been so wet in my life. I gave a sudden gasp as he stretched me, rocking my hips back and pressing my feet against the floor. He groaned as he pushed up into my tightness, filling me in a way that made me heady, sliding in almost to the root. He shuffled closer on his knees, his hips moving up between my thighs, making me open for him even more.

He lowered himself on his forearms, coming all the way down until his chest was scraping my breasts, and began to thrust in slow waves, not wanting to hurt me. I felt him move deep...*deeper* and the sensations had me squeezing my eyes shut and biting on the edge of my thumb. The thickness of him, spreading my slickened walls; the heat of him, throbbing so deep inside me. We were both sweating now, from the sun and from what we were doing, our skin shining glossily. Each thrust was a little deeper...and then, when his hips pushed forward for the fourth time, I felt the hardness of his groin kiss up against my lips, and I knew I'd taken all of him.

He paused there for a second, kissing me, and the feel of his tongue deep in my mouth, when his cock was so deeply buried inside me, was incredible. The size of his body as he hulked over me made me weak. His chest and shoulders blocked out most of the sky. I felt like some maiden, ravished by a god.

He started up a rhythm, moving faster, now. The concrete was hard under my bare ass, but the warm scratchiness of it felt good. Where I normally would have bucked and swirled my hips and fucked him back, I was forced to pin myself to the ground, lying there passively as he fucked me. It was a new experience for me, being so still. I'm not a shrinking violet when it comes to sex but now I had to be like some Victorian lady on her wedding night, staring at the ceiling and thinking of England.

Only I was staring into the most gorgeous pair of blue Irish eyes ever, and I most definitely wasn't thinking of England. I was focusing on every exquisite pull and slide of his cock inside me, every grind of his groin against my clit. Each touch of his chest on my nipples shot fire through me. And it was all happening outdoors, where I could feel the breeze waft against my toes and the sun beat down on my bare legs. There was nothing I could do except lie there and take it all in.

As he sped up, he pushed my legs wider and lifted them a little with his forearms, opening me up more. I felt something change inside me, felt his cock reach some new place, and I let out a little growl of delight.

He leaned right down over me, his mouth close to my ear, and started to talk to me as he fucked me, a filthy litany made even better by his Irish accent. "Oh, you love that, don't you? Being really opened up and fucked, nice and deep? God, I've wanted to do this to you for so long. In the ring. In the diner. Even at The Pit. And when your clothes were wet and I could see those perfect tits."

The words flared and glowed inside my brain, feeding the growing heat.

"This is only the beginning, Sylvie. I'm going to fuck you and fuck you and fuck you. Understand?" He slowed his thrusts, punctuating his words with them, his lips drawn back into a grimace as he fought for control. "*Do...you...under...stand?*"

The heat was twisting and thrashing inside me, making my whole body quake. "*Yes!*" I managed. God, I didn't want anything else. I'd escaped. In my mind, I'd escaped my whole shitty life with Rick and The Pit and Alec's injuries. I'd escaped and found paradise and I didn't want it to ever end. We'd find some room somewhere and lock the door and never come out again.

He sped up again, his powerful ass flexing, his thighs driving him into me, so hard and long and thick. I could feel it start and I dug my fingers into his back. Then it was on me and I was grabbing for him, clawing at him, wanting to wrap his whole body into me as the orgasm crashed through me in waves. He kept going, extending it, and only slowed to a stop when I lay still.

I took stock. I was panting and gasping, the echoes of the orgasm still ringing in my head. He was moving inside me just a tiny amount, the way men do when they're still ready.

He was still ready.

I put my hand on his shoulder, marveling at its strength. "I need to go on top," I said, my voice weak and croaky.

And *need* was right. I needed to move. Lying there like a ravished maiden was great, but now I needed to show him how I felt about *him*.

He rolled over onto his back, frowning a little at the hard concrete and then giving me an apologetic look, like, *Oh wow, is this what it was like for you?* And I smiled.

I threw one leg over him, straddling him. He looked up at me and I had a moment of panic as I realized I was opening my legs wide, right in front of him, in broad daylight. It felt weird, feeling the air blowing through the little curls of hair, feeling it cooling the wetness there. Weird, but wonderful. Because he was looking at me with such an expression of pure, undiluted lust that it chased all my fears away.

I knelt with a knee either side of him and put one hand on his chest, unable to stop myself running it over the smooth expanse of his pec. I began to slowly lower myself, using the other hand to bring the throbbing head of him to the lips of my sex. When it touched me, I couldn't help staying there for a moment, just running it back and forth over my folds. He groaned good-naturedly and raised his hips, thinking I was teasing him. But I just wanted to feel him there, so hot and alive and ready.

I sank down on him, closing my eyes and arching my back as he spread me wide and plunged into me. It felt different, now I was the one in control. Bigger, almost—I could feel every inch of him. Wonderfully big.

I slid right down onto him until our bodies met and began to pump myself on top of him, using my legs to power me up and down. His hands went to my waist and he started to help, lifting me a little, but I shook my head. I pushed his hands away...and then pressed them down to the concrete. It was comical, my little hands against his huge wrists—he could easily have batted me away. But he didn't. He just grinned up at me and played along—for now.

I started to fuck him, bouncing up and down, sliding my body along that magnificent cock. Sitting up, I knew my head might be visible above the wall—we'd edged closer to it, when we rolled over. But I didn't care. If someone passing in the street glanced up and saw us, let them watch.

I put both hands on his chest, smoothing them over his muscles as if I was sculpting him. His cock was silk and iron inside me, filling every part of me on each in-thrust, leaving me empty and aching as it slid out. I could feel my shins and knees grinding against the roof—God, I was going to have bruises tomorrow. But I didn't care about that, either.

I sped up, arching my back as the pleasure built and built, feeling the sweat trickling down my spine, feeling it wet on his chest. And now he reached for me, unwilling to be passive any longer. He filled his hands with my breasts and started pinching at my nipples, making me buck and shake atop him. He drew me down into a kiss. My hips went frantic as I fucked and fucked him while he tongue-fucked my mouth and stretched my nipples just enough to—

The climax rocketed through me and exploded. I let go of his chest and grabbed his head, pulling myself closer, gasping and panting into his mouth. My hips pressed hard against him, mashing our groins together. I clenched and spasmed around him and felt his first hot release, followed by another and another. He growled and broke the kiss and bit at my neck as he shot into me, bucking his hips upward so hard he lifted both of us.

And then he slumped down and I slumped on top of him, stretching my legs out. We were both soaked with sweat and aching and probably bruised from the hard roof, and we didn't care at all.

We lay there for a long time, letting the sun dry us, neither of us wanting to think about practicalities like where all our clothes had wound up. I lay with my head on his chest, the warmest and most comfortable pillow I'd ever found in my life. I never wanted to move.

"You're in me, Sylvie," he muttered at last. "In my head. In my feckin' soul. I need you."

I put my arms around him and hugged him tight. "I need you, too," I whispered.

"I don't think I can hit you again," he said.

I pressed my lips tight together. All I wanted was for both of us to walk away from all this. To be two normal people in a normal relationship. Why couldn't we have that? What had we done so wrong, that we deserved this instead?

But being normal wasn't an option for us. "You have to," I told him. "You have to hit me...and more. You have to get me ready. Or I'll die in The Pit."

He went silent for a long time, his arms tightening around me. But eventually, he nodded.

It was only when we'd showered and got into our street clothes and I checked my phone that I found the message. Sent an hour before, just as we were finally breaking down the barriers between us.

It was from Rick. He wanted me to come to The Pit that night.

It was time to meet my opponent.

26

AEDAN

I needed someplace quiet to talk to Sylvie, so I sprang for a cab to take us to The Pit. In the back seat, I held her hand and pep-talked her.

"It's not a fight," I said. "Not really. More of a preview. You'll go a round or two, but no one wants anyone to get badly hurt. It's just a chance for the crowd to see who's coming up in two weeks, so they can start placing bets." The last two words made me sick to my stomach. Rich suits, throwing fistfuls of hundred dollar bills at the unlicensed bookies, betting on who would walk away. Betting on my angel.

She'd never looked more beautiful. The sunset was streaming through the windows of the cab, bathing everything in fire. She looked so small and fragile, sitting there in her tank top and sweatpants. She'd been so nervous, I'd had to remind her to bring something to put on over the top, because it would get cold once the sun went down. Now she clutched the hooded top in her hands, scrunching the fabric between them.

"It's normal," I told her. "Rick does it whenever it's a brand new fighter." *So why hadn't I seen it coming?* I felt like an idiot. I was meant to be preparing her for all this and I'd completely missed it. I'd been too busy laying her down on the damn rooftop.

Our whole relationship had just seismically shifted and, thanks to Rick, we didn't even have time to talk about it. Maybe that was for the best. I never was much good at talking.

I quit beating myself up long enough to think about tactics. Should we pretend she hadn't been training? Lull them into a false sense of security? Rick knew me. If he saw me, would he guess I'd been training her?

Should I stay away, so that Rick didn't suspect? Part of me thought I should. Another part wondered if that was just an excuse, and I just couldn't bear to see her get hurt.

No. No way. I couldn't leave her alone now. I was going to be there, every step of the way.

And there was another reason to be there. I'd come up with a plan, something that might just get Sylvie out of the fight altogether. It was the last thing I wanted to do, but if it saved her from fighting...

I squeezed her hand and she smiled at me, hiding her fear.

I smiled back, doing the same.

27

SYLVIE

I t was a smaller crowd, but meaner. The hangers-on didn't get told about events like this. Only the hardcore, the ones who bet serious money, got the discreet text message telling them there was fresh meat to view.

I took a deep breath and walked towards the door, trying to look nonchalant. But The Pit had never been a welcoming place for women and what happened to me last time I was there made it even harder. Stepping out of the twilight and into the dark, warm interior was like stepping into hell...especially since I'd soon be heading down to the lower level. *Nothing like that's going to happen this time,* I told myself. Except that, in some ways, this would be worse. My near-rape was something I could be saved from. This fight—that Aedan reassured me wouldn't involve me actually getting hurt—was something that *had* to happen.

I was hoping I could pass unnoticed in the crowd, hoping that everyone would presume I was just the girlfriend of some spectator until the actual fight. Everything, I realized, would depend on whether Rick had hinted to the audience what would be different about these fighters. If they knew they were coming to see women....

It was obvious as soon as we neared the balcony around the pit.

Heads turned, as if they could smell my feminine scent. A sort of rumble went through the crowd, expanding outward from where Aedan and I stood.

He put an arm around my waist and pulled me closer.

I could see their eyes eating me up. Wondering if I would be the victim or the victor...and, from their sneers, the answer seemed obvious. Had they already seen the other woman? Or did I just look so weak that I'd crumble before *any* opponent?

There was another look, too. The one I'd been aware of before, but that held new fear for me after last time. That hungry, male look, so different to the looks Aedan gave me, even when he was fucking me. It was a look with no warmth at all, no interest in my happiness or my pleasure. It was a look that stripped off my clothes and spread me open.

Legs shaking, I let Aedan lead me downstairs.

Rick was there with Al and Carl, his two bodyguards. He looked to be in a good mood, his cane shining extra-bright as if he'd polished it specially.

And behind him, leaning against a wall, was a woman.

I don't know what I'd expected. A six foot Amazonian, maybe, like some barbarian queen minus the broadsword and armor. Or maybe an Asian kung fu expert all dressed in black. But she was nothing like either of those.

She was about the same height as me. In places, she looked thinner. In others, she was carrying more muscle. She had long brown hair in dreadlocks and skin as pale as mine. I frowned, trying to figure it out. Rick would have wanted to find someone to destroy me. Had he gone to the semi-pro circuit? She looked ripped, but not in an athletic, glowing-with-health way. Or was she the girlfriend or even sister of someone else who owed him a debt—my counterpart? What if she had some powerful reason to win, too? What if one of *her* loved ones' lives depended on it?

"Sylvie," said Rick with a cat-like grin. "Meet Jacki."

I wasn't sure what I was supposed to do. Shake her hand? I gave her a tentative smile. She scowled at me.

I looked down at what I was wearing—sweatpants, sneakers and a tank top. I looked as if I was ready to get in the ring. Jacki wore jeans and a t-shirt. She didn't look like a trained fighter. What was going on?

"I had some trouble, finding someone for you to fight," said Rick, as if he'd done us a huge favor. "Had to really dig around. But then someone suggested Jacki and all my problems were solved. Jacki was happy to come down here and hand your ass to you for cash, and a shot at the winner's bonus. Weren't you, Jacki?"

Jacki spat on the floor. "Bitch, you better not start crying the first time that pretty face hits the floor. We gotta give people a show."

And then I saw the gang tattoos on her neck and I understood.

Aedan stepped forward out of the shadows. "This is supposed to be boxing," he growled. "Bare knuckle boxing. Not feckin' street fighting."

Rick turned. *"Aedan?"* His face went through a complex series of emotions. Fear. Anger. Suspicion. It was the first time I'd ever seen him really shaken. His bodyguards stepped forward protectively. *What the hell's going on?* I knew that Aedan used to be a fighter and I'd figured out that Rick used to manage him, just like he managed Alec. But this was something else—the relationship between them was a lot more complex.

And then Aedan said something that made me forget everything else.

"I'll fight," he said. "I'll fight instead of Sylvie."

28

SYLVIE

F or once, Rick and I both had the same reaction. "*What?!*" we both said at the same time.

"I'll fight." Aedan pointed at me. "Instead of her. Call off the girl fight. It'll be me against whatever guy Alec was going to fight."

Rick seemed to relax a little. He'd looked scared, before, but the balance of power had subtly shifted, now. "You're fucking her," he muttered, glancing at me. "Interesting."

I saw Aedan tense up. I realized Rick now had leverage over him. But why was Rick so scared of him in the first place? What had happened between these two?

"I'll fight!" Aedan snapped. "Me instead of her!"

Rick glanced between us, considering it. My heart jumped into my mouth. Had Aedan been planning this, without telling me? Was it possible Rick would accept? The idea of Aedan in the pit, with some thug pounding at his face, made me sick. This was my problem—I couldn't let someone else take it on for me. But I'd be lying if I said that there wasn't a small part of me that prayed for Rick to say *yes*. This whole nightmare could be over for me in a heartbeat.

"No," said Rick. "Tempting, but I don't have anyone I could put up against you. You'd beat the hell out of anyone I could get." Then he grinned. All his usual confidence had returned. "Besides, it's good to try new things. You've had your day. It's time to try women. The crowd seems pretty excited."

Aedan glared at him. "You *fecker!* It's not right!"

Rick shrugged. "Wasn't my idea. It was Sylvie's. Anyway, times change. Women are always saying they want equality. Well, here it is." He grinned a crocodile's grin at Jacki and me. From her sneer, I suspected she felt much the same way about him that I did.

He stalked out into the pit, brandishing his cane, and the crowd roared. Aedan pulled me away from Jacki and into a corner. His whole body was rigid with tension.

"What was *that?*" I demanded. "You were going to take my place? When were you going to tell me?"

He stared at me angrily. "I don't want to see you get hurt!"

We glared at each other for a moment and then I softened, seeing the worry in his eyes. His plan hadn't worked, anyway, so it was irrelevant. And I loved him for trying. I put my arms around him and hugged him close.

He squeezed me back. Then I felt the tension return to his body and he whispered in my ear. "This is bad," he said. "I've been teaching you boxing. She's used to handing out beat downs in the street. It's going to be dirty."

He sounded worried and that scared the crap out of me. "OK, so...what do I do?" I looked up into his eyes, ready to absorb as much as I could as fast as I could.

"...I have no idea," he said at last.

"*What?*"

"I never fought a woman!" he snapped. "If it was *boxing* then it doesn't make any feckin' difference—a woman's just like a smaller man. But she'll fight like she fights on the street. That's completely different."

My heart was suddenly pounding. This was much, much worse than anything I'd prepared myself for. *I might as well not have trained at all.* Out in the pit, Rick seemed to be coming to the end of his speech. We had seconds. I started to panic-breathe.

Aedan grabbed my shoulders. "OK, look. If it was a man, he'd try to bite and gouge. So keep clear of her teeth and be ready to block her when she scratches at you. And a man would try to knock you down and pin you so he could finish you off, so stay on your feet."

"Okay," I said breathlessly.

"It's not all bad," he said. "She probably hasn't been trained. She'll be undisciplined. Unbalanced. Keep your guard up and look for a weakness. Remember you're an out-boxer—keep your distance."

"Okay," I said again.

In the pit, we could hear Rick giving it everything he had. *"From the mean streets of New York City!"* he bellowed. "Raised by a junkie mom and a deadbeat dad, she started selling her body at fourteen. She beat up girls who tried to steal her turf and now she lays down the law in a gang. *Jacki!"*

I saw Jacki roll her eyes and wondered how much of that story Rick had made up. But she stalked out into the pit to huge cheers.

"Just stay focused," said Aedan, rubbing my shoulders. "Don't panic. Don't drop your guard."

"And from the Upper West Side!" Rick yelled.

What? I wasn't from the Upper West Side. Even when Dad was alive, even when *Mom* was alive, we were still poor.

"She was society's *it girl,"* Rick told the crowd. "Pampered and privileged. Sent to a Swiss finishing school to learn manners, where rumor has it she fucked half her male teachers. Then to Harvard, where she studied law..."

The crowd growled. Everybody hated lawyers.

"But then she fell from grace!"

The crowd roared their approval.

"Unable to resist the bad boy charm of her very first criminal client, she eloped with him...only to be dumped by the roadside. Disowned by her wealthy family, desperate for money...*now she's here!"*

The crowd went wild. I exchanged disbelieving looks with Aedan, feeling sick. Not only had he made up a ridiculous story for me—and probably for Jacki, too—but he'd set her up as the underdog and me as the wealthy, snobby girl who needed teaching a lesson.

It was clear who the crowd would want to win.

"Sylvie!" yelled Rick.

Aedan grabbed me and kissed me hard. Then he lifted his fists towards mine. I realized he wanted me to tap fists with him. The same good luck ritual I used to do with Alec. I stared at his huge, scarred hands and at my own much smaller ones, and then I tapped.

And ran out into the pit before I could change my mind.

29

SYLVIE

I'd watched plenty of fights from the balcony. And I'd been down in the side room, where Aedan now was, when Alec fought. So I thought I knew what to expect.

I was wrong.

The crowd above became a hooting, screaming hurricane, their voices surrounding me and leaving my ears ringing. The harsh overhead lights blinded me whenever I looked up, turning the people above into faceless silhouettes. I could just see the white of their teeth and the gleam of their spit as they yelled.

The pit itself was a merciless prison. Smooth concrete walls much higher than my head. A bare concrete floor. The doors into the side rooms looked pathetically small.

There was nowhere to run.

Jacki was already standing directly across from me, glaring at me. Rick slapped me enthusiastically on the shoulder and ran back to the side room to wait with Aedan.

And the fight began.

Jacki started to circle around to the side and I did the same, walking like a crab, hands raised to guard myself in case she suddenly came at me. *I'm not ready!* My heart was thumping in my chest and I could actually see my hands shaking as I held them in front of me. This wasn't like the ring I'd trained in—*at all!* There was no bounce in the floor, no give. If I even slipped and went down, it was going to hurt. If I was knocked down and hit my head...it didn't bear thinking about.

Jacki suddenly came at me in a zig-zagging, erratic run. Her hands weren't up in fists. They were more like hooked claws, ready to grab and pull and tear.

I backed up, trying to keep my distance. Immediately, she moved faster. It was obvious which of us had the upper hand, right from the start. I was scared of her but she wasn't scared of me.

She suddenly snaked her hand out and I blocked instinctively. But she wasn't trying to hit me. She grabbed my hand and *pulled,* using the full weight of her body to swing me around. My feet skittered under me and my stomach lurched. The wall came up to meet me, too fast—

I crashed into the concrete, feeling the gritty surface chew at my exposed arm and shoulder. My hip banged hard against it and my leg went numb.

The crowd cheered.

I tried to get away from her, but I was staggering, now, and didn't have the speed to get any distance. All I could do was retreat, backing up along the curving wall, praying I didn't trip over my own feet. If I went down, it was all over.

I didn't dare take my eyes off Jacki's cruelly grinning face. But then I saw the door to the side room behind her and, in it, Aedan. He was screaming at me.

Screaming *hit her.*

Before I could take it in, she grabbed me again. This time, she pulled me towards her and—

Pain exploded in my face. I tasted and smelled blood. And suddenly it was fountaining out of me, splotching onto my top. I lifted my hands to my face and they instantly turned red. Jesus, what had she done to me?

The pain dulled a little, centering on my nose. I realized she'd head-butted me, and my nose was bleeding.

For the first time, I started to pick out voices in the crowd.

"Get her on the ground!"

"Shove your foot up the bitch!"

"Fucking finish her!"

She was coming at me again, hands raised, leg drawn back.

Hit her.

She was going to grab me and kick me.

Hit her.

She was going to get me down on the ground and smash my face into the floor, just like she promised.

Hit her. Behind Jacki, I saw Aedan screaming it.

I can't! And then Jacki shouted and came at me hard, hands grabbing for my waist—

I lashed out and two solid weeks of muscle memory snapped into place. There was a sickening crack as my fist hit Jacki's jaw. Her head snapped to the side and she staggered. The crowd cheered even louder. Apparently, it didn't matter who got hit, as long as someone did.

Jacki put her hand to her face and winced, then looked at me, her eyes narrowed. I was looking at my own fist in wonder. My knuckles were throbbing, my wrist aching. *Did I really just hit her?* I realized I'd dropped my guard and started to lift my hands again.

Too late.

Jacki shoulder-charged me and bore us both down to the floor. I landed under her, gasping as the air was knocked out of me. Jacki's expression was vicious, now, her lips drawn back from her teeth in an animal snarl.

I lifted my head, only to have her punch me. It wasn't as strong as one of my punches—it seemed like she was used to grabbing and throwing, not hitting. But it sent my head towards the concrete and I only just managed to hold it away, my neck muscles screaming. She hit me again, on the other side, and this time it hurt more.

"Tear her clothes off!" screamed someone in the crowd. There was a sudden roar of approval from all around the room.

Sickened, I looked up at Jacki. She looked equally appalled, her nose wrinkling in distaste. But then she glanced off to the side.

Towards Rick.

I couldn't see him, but he must have nodded. Jacki punched me a third time and then grabbed my tank top at the base of one strap and jerked. The strap tore free and suddenly my bra and breasts were revealed to the crowd. The hoots and wails were deafening. Jacki's hands reached for me again—

A shining aluminum cane shot between us, then pushed her back. She got off me, sullen-faced, holding her jaw. Already, the skin there was starting to discolor. The crowd howled their disapproval as they realized the fight was over.

"That's all, folks!" yelled Rick. "That was just a taster. If you want to see Sylvie get hers, be here! Same place! Same time! Two weeks!" And he grabbed Jacki's hand and raised it in the air in victory.

She grinned at the crowd and then scowled down at me. I clutched the rags of my tank top to my chest, humiliated and shaking. In those final few seconds, all of the crowd's male rage had bubbled up to the surface and shown itself for what it really was. And it looked like Jacki and Rick were only too happy to go along with it, if it kept them happy.

Aedan ran over. For a second, he stood there glaring at Rick, his massive fists bunched, clearly ready to kill him. Al and Carl sidled up to protect their boss but, for a second, it looked as though Aedan was going to wade in regardless.

I reached up and grabbed Aedan's hand. "Just get me out of here?" I pleaded.

With a last snarl at Rick, Aedan pulled me to my feet and helped me to the side room. My legs had turned to jelly and I had to lean on him the whole way. I felt slightly better once we were out of sight of all those male eyes.

"Let me look at you," he said. He took my head between his hands, his eyes wide with fear. He probed gently at my nose and I squealed and thumped him on the arm. "Sorry," he said. "But good news—it's not broken. Just bleeding. Put pressure on it and it'll stop." He examined my cheeks and then my hip. "Nothing too bad here, either—just bruises."

Just bruises? I wanted to burst into tears. The adrenaline was receding and the pain was hitting me full force, now. My whole body throbbed and I wanted to crawl under a rock and die. "I'm sorry," I blurted.

He stared at me. "*Sorry?* What have you got to be sorry about?"

I was breathing in big gulps now. It felt like I was about to start crying, but the hot explosion of tears didn't arrive. I was stuck in the prickly-faced heaving stage that normally precedes it. "I—I couldn't hit her. I didn't know what to do. I messed up."

"*Messed up?!*" He hugged me close. "You did *great*. Neither of us was ready for *that*. But now we can be. We know what she's got. I can teach you how to deal with that, how to fight dirty. She can't learn to fight like you—not in a couple of weeks." He squeezed me tighter and stroked the back of my hair. "It's okay. It's all going to be okay."

Now I *did* start to cry. I cuddled in tight against his chest, my face leaving blood on his t-shirt.

"And you *did* hit her. Christ, you nearly broke her jaw!"

I gave a nervous little laugh, but I didn't feel like laughing. It had all been way too frightening: the brutal aggression; the speed at which it had all gone wrong, when she'd charged me; the cruel, male evil of the crowd at the end.

I pushed back from Aedan. "Take me home," I begged.

He nodded and passed me the hooded top I'd brought with me. I pulled it on over my ruined tank top and we headed for the stairs.

30

AEDAN

I pushed through the crowd, acting as a wedge to keep them clear of Sylvie. They weren't so brave, now that they were face-to-face with her...and me. It was impossible to tell which of the men had yelled the worst things. But all of them were guilty. All of them had, at a minimum, come along and watched. None of them had left in disgust when Jacki had torn off Sylvie's top.

I was ready to kill every single one of them.

I settled for battering them aside, using plenty of elbow and shoulder, and growling at any who resisted. Outside, I bundled Sylvie into a cab and told the cabbie to take us to my place.

I looked at Sylvie. "No arguments," I said. "I don't want you to be alone, tonight."

She nodded.

At my apartment, I showed her to the shower. "Get in," I said. "Take your time. I'll get us something to eat." What I really wanted was to do something nice for her—some big bath filled with bubbles and scented candles and all that girly shit. But I didn't have any of those things. All I had to offer her was hot water and men's shower gel. And yet she looked at me as if I'd done all that and more.

I left her alone to shower. The thought of her naked in there had me instantly hard in my pants but she'd been through too much—I didn't want to do anything that would make her feel pressured into sex, not right now. So I retreated to the living room and ordered a massive pizza with everything on, and dug some cold beers out of the refrigerator.

When the bathroom door inched open, it was like a rerun of that time she'd fallen in the river...but so much had changed, since then. She stared at me around the edge of the door, steam billowing out around her, and I stared right back at her.

Her nose had stopped bleeding and she'd washed the blood away, but she was still red and tender there. Her left cheek had a dark bruise where Jacki's fist had cracked across it and her right eye was turning purple, the lid swollen.

Her lip was trembling and her eyes were filled with tears. "How do I..." She swallowed. "How do I look?"

And I realized that she hadn't seen herself, yet. The mirror in the bathroom broke a long time ago, after I—

Well. It broke.

The only mirror is in the living room, and she couldn't see it from where she was. And I'd hustled her straight through to the bathroom when we arrived. She hadn't seen the damage, yet.

"It's not so bad," I told her. I got up slowly and walked across to her, grabbing the best towel I had. She hesitantly released her grip on the door and I slowly opened it and wrapped the towel around her like a dress.

I guided her to the mirror, stepping behind her and wrapping my arms around her waist for support. Her steps got smaller and smaller as she approached. When she saw her face, I saw her go pale. I thought she was going to be sick.

"It'll heal," I told her as she touched her cheek. *She's never been hurt before, you feckin' idiot,* I told myself. I was used to coming home with a broken nose or a mashed-up lip, back in the day. But she'd always known the same face in the mirror. Now it had suddenly changed. She must not feel like *her* anymore.

I lifted my arms and wrapped them tighter around her, hugging her close to my chest. "You're beautiful," I told her.

She shook her head and I heard her breath catch. She was on the edge of tears.

"*Beautiful,*" I said. And she was. It broke my heart to see her hurt like this. But it didn't for one second change the way I felt about her.

And for the first time, I felt that deep lurch inside, the one where you feel like the floor's just been pulled out from under you. I'd been thinking about how much I wanted her, but I'd been skating around the other stuff: how much I liked talking to her; how she made me laugh like no one else did; how I'd wanted to protect her from the first moment I met her.

No. No way. Jesus, look at me—look at my shitty apartment. Look at what I am. She deserves a hell of a lot better than me.

She turned around, wincing as she moved her hip. "Thank you," she whispered. And she drew me down into a soft, tender kiss. And for a little while, I let my doubts go and allowed myself to pretend we could actually be together, long term.

I could feel her naked body through the towel, cool and deliciously soft against me. But before things went any further, there was something I needed to do. I picked her up and lifted her onto the bed on her back. Then I unwrapped the towel, leaving her naked.

Her eyes widened.

I held up my hands in defense. "I'm not—Not *that.* I gotta check the rest of you."

She looked chastened...and a little disappointed. "Oh."

The way she said it made my cock twitch and strain against my thigh. Damn, but this girl turned me on. "Not that we can't do that too," I growled.

Her voice changed again, a nervous little laugh creeping in. "Oh!"

I looked down at her. The most gorgeous girl I'd ever seen, naked on my bed, and I had to be halfway professional, at least until I'd checked her over. I took a look at her hip, where she'd whacked it against the wall. There was one hell of an ugly bruise there, purple and green and spreading to cover an area the size of my hand. *Ouch.*

I took her ankle in my hand and tried lifting her leg a little, then bending it. She winced, but everything seemed to move okay. I'd been worried she might have fractured something. I tried rotating the joint a little and that seemed okay, too.

It was difficult to ignore the fact that I'd just opened her legs, and that her naked pussy was right there in front of me.

We stared at one another.

She pressed her thighs together. "I want to," she said quietly. "But I'm not sure I can. I'm too banged up."

I nodded quickly. "Gotcha." And I started to cover her up. Then I saw her blink a couple of times, not quite crying but on the verge. She thought I didn't want to. She wasn't up to sex, but she needed that reassurance. She needed to know that I still found her beautiful.

"There is something we can do," I said. "Without you moving."

"Oh yeah?" she asked softly. "What?"

I opened the towel again. Her legs were still a little way apart. I climbed onto the bed and lowered my head between her thighs.

She drew in a huge, startled gasp of air as my tongue touched her lips and flicked up the line between them. I'd always loved going down on a woman and Sylvie had the sweetest, most perfect pussy of them all. Up on the roof had been great but here, with her lying on a bed, I could really go to town.

I had to be careful to avoid touching her hip, or moving her legs. I didn't want any pain to distract from the pleasure. I slid my hands up to her breasts and began to gently stroke them, and she groaned. God, they felt so good under my palms, full and soft and with the nipples already hardening to warm, stiff buds between my fingers.

I traced the shape of each lip again and again, staying clear of her clit for now. I listened to her breathing and felt her movements under my hands. Only when she was panting and gasping and grinding her head into the pillow did I flick my tongue over the hidden little nub for the first time. I closed my mouth around it and sucked and she went wild.

Very slowly, I parted her folds with a finger and then slid it up into her. God, the warm, silken pressure of her around me, so smooth and perfect. I began to pump slowly at her while I wrote the alphabet with my tongue on her clit.

I heard her grab the headboard of the bed. Her breathing was coming fast, now, and I could feel her thighs twitching. She was instinctively moving to lock them closed around my head, but her banged-up hip was forcing her to keep them open. In a way, that made it even better. That little bit of helplessness, the fact she had to just surrender to my mouth.

I added a second finger and curled them into her until I found that secret place that made her groan low in her throat and arch her back. My tongue moved faster, sliding over her clit again and again, taking her higher and higher, then pulling back just before she could reach the summit. I teased her like that for a half hour, until she writhed and cried out my name and finally clawed at my shoulders and begged me. Only then did I speed up my fingers, fucking her deep and circling that secret spot. Only then did I go crazy on that firm little nub, lashing it with my tongue and this time not stopping. Only then did I take her nipples between finger and thumb and pinch....

She came, rocking the bed and banging the headboard against the wall, her whole body going tense as a bowstring. I felt the shudders run through her, loving the way she arched her back and pushed her breasts up into my hands, the way her pussy contracted around my fingers. At the very end, I moved up the bed and kissed her, my fingers still inside her, feeling the last tremors squeeze me even as she panted against my lips.

Seconds later, the door buzzer went and I rewrapped her in the towel and left her cuddled there while I paid the pizza guy. We found a position that was comfortable for her—me sitting up in the bed with her between my legs and lying back against my chest—and I fed her pizza like that, and we drank cold beers and watched late-night TV until the early hours.

31

SYLVIE

I yawned and stretched and looked at the ceiling, trying to remember where I was.

Aedan. Aedan's place. And then the pain returned, throbbing from my hip and my cheeks, and it all came back to me.

He was still sleeping, spooning me from behind. The feel of his naked body against mine was incredible—hard, warm muscle kissing up against my back, nestled against every inch of me from shoulder to ankle. I wanted to never move. But I had to see.

I gently lifted his arm off me and slipped out of bed. In the half-light of dawn, I checked the mirror.

Eurgh! The bruises seemed to have gotten darker overnight, finishing their parade of colors to settle on ugly purples and greens. The one on my hip was the worst, but at least that would be covered up. My face, though....

I knew I couldn't show up for work like this. What the hell would I say—that I'd been mugged? I couldn't be around hotel guests with my face all banged up. My manager would be outwardly sympathetic, but would quietly stop giving me shifts. I'd be branded as *trouble*. I'd have to call in sick, instead.

No one at the hotel knew what was going on. I'd told them only that my brother was ill, and that I needed to look after him. A few of the other maids had asked what was happening with me, commenting that I looked different since I'd started training. I'd been tempted to confide in them but, every time I opened my mouth, I'd stopped. There just seemed to be a yawning gulf between their safe little world—the one I used to inhabit—and mine. The only people I felt close to, now, were Aedan and my sleeping brother. And the doctor at the hospital, Heather. She'd spent more time with me than she probably had time for, sitting next to me while I held Alec's hand. If I came through this, I really owed her a thank you.

If I came through it.

I was walking back to the bed when I heard it. A hard tap at the window, as if someone wanted to come in.

We were five floors up.

I stared at the ragged curtain that covered the glass. The sound came again. Something hard was banging against the pane. A tree? We were right by the docks—there wasn't a tree for miles.

I moved right up to the window, putting my arm over my naked breasts. I told myself it must be a washing line or a cable or something, swaying in the wind, and tugged the curtain back.

A face stared back at me, pressed right up against the other of the glass. Snow white, with two gleaming, beady eyes. I froze.

It opened its mouth and screeched at me. I screamed and staggered back, knocking the back of my legs against the bed and landing on Aedan's sleeping form. He grunted. Outside, the monster was battering at the glass, screeching and....

...flapping?

"Oh," said Aedan, sitting up. "You've met."

The thing was still staring at me through the glass. I grabbed the covers and wound them around me. "*What is it?*"

He looked bemused. "It's a seagull."

"That's not a seagull! It's the size of a—a—" I tried to think of a big bird. A vulture? A buzzard? "It's a freakin' pterodactyl!"

"Yeah, I think its mother slept with an albatross or something." He got up and walked over to the window, completely at home in his nakedness, and opened it. The gull—or whatever the hell it was—gave a last screech of satisfaction and then quieted down. It eyed me.

Hungrily.

"It's kind of sad," said Aedan. "His wing's weak on one side—I think he must have been in a fight or something. He can fly, but not fast. So whenever the other birds see food, he always gets there last and there's nothing left." He dug around in an old pizza box and found a crust, then threw it to the bird. It snapped it out of the air and gulped it down without chewing, then screeched for more.

I was calming down a little, now. The thing was still huge and ugly and looked like it wanted to eat me, but it seemed satisfied with pizza...for now. I stood up and gingerly approached. "So how does he survive?" I asked. "If he can't get any food, then—" I looked at Aedan. "Wait. Do you feed him?"

He flushed.

"Do you feed him *every morning?*" I was incredulous and delighted.

"Not *every* morning," he said testily. "I mean..." His shoulders slumped. "Yeah, okay. Every morning."

The gull shrieked happily and devoured another crust.

"Aedan O'Harra, you *big pile of squidgy goo!* You have a *pet!*"

He'd gone beet red. "It's just a bird."

I threw my arms around him and hugged him hard. There *was* a softer side to him. He just hid it very, very well. "You're just a big softie," I told him, my face buried in his chest.

"I'm addicted to hopeless causes, that's what I am," he grumbled. But he hugged me even harder.

Aedan asked if I wanted to take a day off. "You just had your first fight," he told me. "It's fine."

I knew he was saying it out of concern and that made it even harder because I really, really wanted to. Nothing sounded better than just crawling back into bed and hiding my face from the world.

But if I did that, I knew there was a real chance I'd never come out again. I'd lost the fight and only been saved by Rick, wanting to preserve the finale for the main event. Next time, there wouldn't be any such escape. Next time, I had to win or most likely die.

And that was another problem. I had no intention of killing anyone, but the fight would go on until one of us couldn't get up. Jacki was determined—she wouldn't go down easily and she wouldn't stay down. How hard would I have to hit her, to take her out of the fight? How close would I have to get to killing her? One little mistake, one hard knock of her head against the floor or the wall and I'd be a murderer.

None of this was going to go away. It would all still be waiting for me the next day and the next. So the sooner I got on with things, the better. I only had fourteen days until the fight, now. I couldn't afford to waste one of them.

No one at the gym seemed fazed by my bruises and black eye—if anything, they were still freaked out by the fact I was a woman. And yet, gradually, I was starting to fit in. Maybe it was the sheer volume of time I'd spent there over the previous two weeks, but I felt like I was accepted there, now. Men would nod hello to me when I came in the door. The looks they gave me were respectful—I was one of them. Sure, there were some lecherous glances, but they felt like clean, healthy lust, not that cruel, twisted version the guys at The Pit gave me.

Aedan went easy on me: punches on the light bag and then the heavy bag, some pad work, some speed exercises. We didn't do any sparring. We hadn't been in the ring together since he'd taken me down. Funny, how that had happened only the previous afternoon— it seemed like a lifetime ago.

I knew he was avoiding it. Before everything had gone right with the sex, everything had gone horribly wrong—not just him accidentally whacking me in the side but my complete failure to be able to hit him. I still wasn't sure I was going to be able to and, unless I could, we weren't going to be able to move on with my training. We also needed to change things up and teach me what I needed to know to beat Jacki, now that we knew what we were up against. Dirty fighting, with kicking, grabbing and gouging.

As the day went on, though, I realized what he was doing: he was building my confidence. Giving me easy stuff to do so that I'd forget how badly I'd lost the fight. Hell, it had only been meant to be a warm-up, something to excite the crowd, and I'd still wound up on my back, bruised and bloody, with my top torn off.

And I'd had all the advantages. I didn't know how much of Jacki's background Rick had made up for the crowd, but it was obvious that she'd learned her moves on the street, not in a gym. I'd had two weeks of solid training—she'd just walked in there unprepared. The difference was, she was tough and I wasn't. She'd been fighting in her everyday life for years. I was a goddamn tourist in this world.

Now that she'd seen me, she'd raise her game, too. I remembered that look of surprise when I'd gotten my one good hit in on her. She'd be prepared, next time.

The hell with building up confidence. I hit that bag as hard as I could.

We were doing *two hundred punches, then ten crunches,* which was one of Aedan's sadistic favorites. The repetitiveness of it gave me a chance to think...about us.

Us. Just the previous morning, I'd never have imagined using that word about Aedan and me; now, I couldn't imagine using any other.

What the hell had happened? Apart from the obvious, which was that he'd taken me up on the roof and fucked seven shades of hell out of me. My knees still weakened when I remembered it. This man drove me crazy, with his eyes and his warm, muscled arms that could wrap around me just right and that accent that turned anything into poetry. And now we were together, in some ill-defined way. It didn't feel casual, like two friends who drunkenly sleep together and then just move on. It felt very, very *un*-casual, but was that just me? What was *he* expecting to happen, now? Why hadn't we talked about it?

Actually, I knew the answer to that one. Because we were both scared we were going to mess this whole thing up. It wasn't just the usual relationship nerves. We both knew something was wrong.

The sexual tension had been building for weeks. I'd felt it on my side and I'd thought I'd felt it from Aedan, too. So why had it taken him this long? He didn't strike me as a guy who was nervous about going after what he wanted. The polar opposite, in fact.

He'd held back because of something else, some deep-seated fear about us getting together. What worried me was that I wasn't sure he'd conquered it. It felt more like our feelings had just reached the level where they submerged it. But it was still there, lurking in the depths.

What would happen when it surfaced?

32

AEDAN

I watched her pound the bag: hair pulled back into a ponytail, little beads of sweat rolling down her back between her shoulder blades. I'd wanted her to go easy, today, but she was hitting the bag as if she saw Rick's face on it. She was hurting inside, burning with the frustration of losing. Asking herself what had gone wrong, beating herself up for every little mistake.

I knew the feeling because I'd been there myself. Every fighter had, the first time they lost. In some ways, it's a rite of passage. Some people even say it's better to lose your first than win your first, so you don't get cocky.

But none of that applied to Sylvie. She wasn't a professional fighter and didn't want to become one. She was doing this to save her brother, nothing more. And yesterday's defeat had thrown everything into jeopardy. Tomorrow, we had to get on with training. But she wasn't going to be able to get her head in the game until I got her in a better mood.

She needed a break. Something that would make her feel good.

As if in answer, I glanced down at the swells of her breasts under her Lycra top. My cock swelled and thickened.

Not *that*. Not yet, at least. She needed something....

The word felt alien in my mind. Something *romantic.*

I'd seen, over the last few weeks, how she never got to do anything girly. All she ever wore were jeans and t-shirts. Her hotel shifts barely left time to go out, so she wasn't hanging out with her girlfriends, chatting about...I don't know, guys and... what *do* girls talk about, anyway? Whatever. She wasn't getting that. She'd been surviving, these last few years with her brother. Not living.

She needed to live for a night.

I knew, deep down, that it was a mistake. I knew the sex had been a mistake, and that the smartest thing I could do was end this thing before we got in any deeper. She still thought I was a hero—what would happen when she realized the truth?

But I couldn't stop thinking about those eyes, those lips. I was feckin' addicted to her. And so, however stupid it was, part of me still wanted the fantasy. I still wanted to be with her.

The only problem was, I had no clue what to do. I hadn't been on a date in years. I didn't *do* dates. I fucked and was gone by morning.

So I called Jasmine.

Connor, the other Irishman who trained at the gym, had charmed his way into the bed of some posh cellist on the Upper West Side. I'd thought it wouldn't last, at first. But, from the few times I'd see them together, they were a cute couple. Anyway, the cellist—Karen—had been to some fancy performing arts school with ballet dancers and actresses and people like that. And one night, on a rare night out for me, I'd run into them all and wound up doing tequila shots. Jasmine had been there. She said she was an actress and I vaguely recognized her from that cop show, *Blue & Red.* And she would have been hard to miss anyway—hourglass body and long red hair. If she hadn't already had a boyfriend, I would have tried my luck.

We got talking and kind of split off into our own little corner for almost an hour. Nothing happened or anything—just friendly chat. But by the time I'd walked her to a cab stand and then waited there with her for a cab, we'd gotten to know each other pretty well. And she'd given me her phone number, "Because you'll need it, someday."

Now I did.

I told Sylvie to take five, found a quiet corner of the gym and dug through my phone for Jasmine's number. She'd entered it herself, complete with a selfie of her pulling a goofy face. She answered on the second ring.

"Hey! Who's this?"

I had her number, but she didn't have mine. I must have come up as "unidentified caller." Would she even remember meeting me? "Ahh...well...." I began.

"Connor! Shit, did it all go wrong? Listen, I warned Karen those were *advanced* tips and to practice on a salami first, so don't blame me if you've got teeth marks—"

"Ah, no," I cut in quickly. "It's Aedan."

"Oh." If there was any embarrassment, it was gone in a second. "The boxer, right?"

"Yeah."

"Who quit because—"

"Yeah." Shit, I must have told her everything. In my memory, it had been a nice, friendly conversation but I must have poured my heart out. Jasmine was that sort of person—easy to talk to. And there *had* been a lot of tequila shots.

She was suddenly all serious. "How's it going, Aedan?

"I need some female advice."

"My middle name. What have you done and who did you do it to, you Irish rascal?"

"Nothing! No one!" God, I was actually blushing. She was always like that—flirty and outrageous and yet somehow innocent at the same time. When I'd met her, I'd thought she was the most spellbinding woman I'd ever met. I'd cursed the fact that she was attached. Now I was glad she had been, because—if there was such a thing as fate—it had been saving me for Sylvie. "It's complicated," I told Jasmine. "There's this girl..." I looked across to where Sylvie stood in the ring. She was meant to be on a break, but she'd started hitting the bag again, determined to squeeze every minute she could out of training. "She's incredible." I was surprised by how my throat caught. "And she's had a really tough time of it, and I just want to do

something nice for her. Like, romantic nice. Something that'll make
her feel...*girly.*" I sighed. "Does that make any sort of sense?"

She told me what to do.

"Really?" I blinked. "It's that simple?"

"It's that simple."

33

SYLVIE

"Where are we going?" I asked for the tenth time. Normally after training I'd be running off to my maid job. Tonight, I'd called in sick rather than show up looking like I'd been in a fight. I'd presumed we'd head back to Aedan's apartment and—hopefully— talk about things. But he'd dragged me in the opposite direction as soon as we'd left the gym and now we were in a shopping street. It was evening, but the day's heat had soaked into the sidewalks and buildings and now it was throbbing slowly out around us, turning the air to soup.

"Down here," he said, checking a map on his phone. "Apparently." He'd changed, after the gym, putting on a blue shirt that matched his eyes. I hadn't even known he *owned* a shirt. Thinking about it, it looked suspiciously new.

We rounded the corner. The next street seemed to be nothing but boutiques.

"There," Aedan said, satisfied. "This must be it."

"*What* must be it?" I was looking around for a bar, or a cheap diner, or maybe a sports club. I wondered if he was taking me to see a fight, as some sort of training exercise.

He took hold of the top of my head and gently turned it to look at the boutiques.

"I don't get it," I said.

"We're going to buy a dress."

"That's ridiculous. You don't have the knees to pull it off." I looked up at him to see what the hell was going on.

"I'm serious," he told me. "I'm buying you a dress. As a gift." I could hear how utterly alien the words felt to him, even though he was trying to make it sound as if he did this every day. I just stood there and blinked at him.

He towed me over to the nearest window. "You'd look great in that one," he said, pointing to something that was all red velvet and laces.

I shook my head—in disbelief, not disapproval, because actually it *was* a pretty awesome dress. "What's got into you?" I asked. "I don't have money for stuff like this."

"I'm buying."

"*You* don't have money for stuff like this! And neither of us have time! I'm fighting Jacki again in two weeks! We need to be training! We need to be planning! We—"

"We need to be taking a break. *Especially* you." He grabbed my hands and held them. "Look. I know you're scared. I know you feel like you've gotta work every hour until the fight, or it'll be all your fault if you lose."

I went to protest...and then realized that he'd described exactly what I'd been feeling.

"I know because I've been there," he said. "I understand. But the fight can't be the only thing in your life or you'll burn out. That's why I had to get you out of the gym."

"But why *this?*" I asked, waving my hand at the store windows. "Why not just take me for a beer?"

"Because you deserve nice things," he said softly.

I stared at him, my heart swelling in my chest. It had been a hell of a long time since I'd worn anything other than jeans. The girly, dress-buying, nail salon side of me had died with my mom. And I hadn't realized how much I'd missed it.

"Okay," I said grudgingly. "But maybe not *that* one. I'm not sure all the laces are...*me.*"

"I kinda like the laces," Aidan said with a wicked grin.

I pulled him to the next store. "How about *this?*" I asked. It was white and long and silky and just about the prettiest thing I'd ever seen.

"That could work," he said, grinning. But he wasn't looking at it as much as he was looking at me—at my own stupid smile. He just wanted me to be happy.

"Aedan?"

"Yeah?"

"Thank you."

When we came out of the store, I had not just the dress but shoes to go with it. The bill would have fed me for a week, which was exactly why I'd barely bought myself any new clothes in the last few years—I hadn't been able to justify it.

And he'd known that, somehow. It was scary, how well he could read me.

I pulled him close, right there in the middle of the sidewalk, and hugged him. It was the first time I'd managed to get Jacki's face out of my head all day. "Thank you," I said again. "It's lovely. I'm not sure where I'll be able to wear it, but—"

"You can wear it right now," he said. "We've got a table booked for eight."

When we came out of the store, I had not just the dress but shoes to

The restaurant wasn't super-posh, thank God. I would have run screaming if it had been. It was friendly, with small tables and lots of candlelight, but still upmarket enough that the dress fit right in. I felt almost glamorous. I was self-conscious about my bruises—my eye, especially, was pretty much impossible to hide with make-up. But most people's attention seemed to be on Aedan. I wasn't surprised. The shirt couldn't hide his muscles. He was imposing as hell, even dressed up. "Are you sure you can afford this?" I asked as we sat down.

"It's no problem. Go nuts." He opened the wine list and his eyes bulged. "Maybe not *too* nuts."

"Do you know the last time I went somewhere where there *was* a wine list?" *Probably before Dad died.* "Seriously—this is great."

It was the best I'd eaten in a long time. After months of noodles and discount breakfast cereal, I'd been getting used to the heavy protein of the boxer's diet. But this was different again: delicately-cooked fish and steamed vegetables, rich sauces and luxuriant desserts.

"You look amazing," he told me.

I grinned. Walking in heels had taken some getting used to again after nothing but sneakers—my legs were going to get their revenge the next morning. But I felt a million miles away from the scared, bruised girl backed into a corner. I'd escaped, just for one night. And Aedan looked so damn gorgeous with his muscled forearms stretching out the fabric of his shirt and those big blue eyes regarding me over the top of his wine glass. I noticed a couple of people eying him up—although, weirdly, they looked almost hostile. *Jealous of me,* I presumed.

The whole dress shopping and dinner thing still had me reeling. After the roof, I'd been worried that he'd only wanted me for sex. But now he was taking me on an actual date.

Something was wrong, though. We'd been happily chatting away for weeks during training but now it felt like everything had changed, and neither of us knew how to act around the other.

"Sorry," he said after a while. "I'm not good at this. I mean, I haven't done it much. Recently." He looked away and rubbed the scars on his neck. *What the hell happened to him?* I wondered. "But I never was good at this stuff. Talking." He grinned suddenly. When he smiled, his whole persona seemed to soften. "Not like Carrick."

I leaned forward eagerly. "You said your brothers were spread out around the country?"

He blinked, as if surprised that I'd remembered that. "Yeah. All over."

"You don't see them?"

He shook his head. "They're better off without me." And the scary thing was how much he obviously believed it.

"Why? Why would you say that?" I reached across the table and took his hand. "Aedan...you're a good guy. What happened to make you think you're not?"

He bent his head and then looked up at me through those heavy brows. For a second, I thought he was going to tell me. Then he shook his head. "Ah, hell. I didn't mean to get into this. Tonight was meant to be about you."

I felt the mood changing. Our wonderful, glamorous night being dragged down into a black, oily sea.

"It can't be that bad," I whispered.

He nodded that it was. I could see the muscles in his shoulders and arms tensing under his shirt, his frustration building. Frustration at what?

"I like you," he said again. "I really do." He was silent for a moment. "But maybe you shouldn't be around me."

I reached across and stroked his cheek. "Why would you say that?"

He sighed and hung his head. I could sense the pressure of it inside him, his past expanding to push away everything good we'd built up. The closer we got, the more he seemed to return to the closed-off man I'd met at The Pit.

I felt as if my heart was made of paper and someone was slowly, cruelly ripping it down the center. I could feel him slipping away and whatever I said didn't seem to make any difference. "Tell me! I like you! I don't care what happened. You're right for me!"

"I'm not right for anyone," he snapped. "And it's not just *what happened*. It's what I am." He glanced around. "Do you know why I've been getting dirty looks all night?"

I looked around us. Everyone was studiously avoiding looking at me. When I caught a waiter's eye, he glanced at Aedan...and yes, I saw his lip curl in distaste.

I'd gotten it wrong, when we walked in. They were all looking at Aedan, but not for the reason I thought. "Why?" I whispered.

The restaurant seemed to grow very quiet, or maybe I was just so focused on his next words that it seemed that way.

"They think I beat you up," he said.

The restaurant, previously so friendly and inviting, became a sea of hostile faces, all staring at us. Judging us. Judging him for raising his fists to me and judging me for taking it and not running to a shelter. *You're enabling him,* the women silently hissed at me. *You're letting him hit you and then letting him buy forgiveness by taking you out to dinner. God, you're pathetic.* A few of them seemed more sympathetic. *She's probably trapped. Co-dependent. Maybe there are kids. Maybe she has nowhere else to go. I wonder if I should say something.*

Everyone so sure they were right.

I stood on shaking legs. Aedan looked up, startled. He seemed to realize what I was going to do just as my mouth opened, but by then even he couldn't have stopped me.

"*HE DOESN'T HIT ME!*" I yelled. The whole room turned to look at us.

"Sylvie—" started Aedan.

"This is my *boyfriend,*" I announced, acid dripping from my words, "and he *doesn't hit me.* I was in a fight, you presumptuous, judgmental *fucks!*"

The room was completely silent. I could hear individual people breathing.

Aedan took out his wallet and counted some bills out onto the table, then stood up and took my hand to lead me towards the door. He was looking at me in total amazement...and respect.

I refused to move for a moment. I grabbed the front of his shirt and pulled him into a deep, long kiss, pressing myself up against his chest. He got over his shock quickly and kissed me back just as hard, his hands going down to my ass.

Only then did I let him lead me outside.

"Thank you," he said, still sounding stunned. "You didn't have to do that."

"I'm not having people think that about you," I told him.

He stared at me sadly. "They're *right*. I don't hit you but I'm just a" —he stared down at his hands—"just a...*thug.*"

"I don't believe that."

"It's still true. I've done stuff that..." He shook his head. "You deserve better. You deserve a good guy."

I could see him fighting with himself. God, what was this thing that was tearing him apart on the inside? He'd brought me out on this date, he obviously wanted to be with me...and now he was pushing me away to protect me.

Well, the hell with that.

I pressed myself close to him again, feeling his warmth. "Maybe a bad guy is what I want. Because I want you."

He took a deep breath and stared off down the street for a long time, not meeting my eyes. When he finally looked back at me, things had changed. He'd come to a decision. He gave me that same hot lick of a look he'd given me when I'd first seen him at The Pit. Then he pushed me back against the nearest wall and kissed me with a raw, breathless intensity. It was as if a dam had broken inside him. He leaned in close. "Okay, then," he muttered. "If that's what you want, Sylvie...that's what you'll get."

34

AEDAN

Her apartment was closer. It was the first time I'd been there—a whole part of her life that I hadn't seen yet. I was on her territory now, bringing all the bad shit that came with me into her world.

But that's what she wanted. And maybe it was finally time to start listening.

We were tearing at each other's clothes even as we came in the door. Sylvie had her hands under my shirt, sliding over my stomach and then around back to trace the muscles there. She pressed herself against my chest, kissing me, barely coming up for air, and I groaned at the way her breasts pillowed against me. I already had my hands on her ass, squeezing the firm cheeks through the silky fabric of her dress, loving the way it slid over her skin. She wriggled against me and her breasts did wonderful things against my chest. *Hell yeah!*

After the summer heat outside, the apartment was blissfully cool from having been unoccupied for a couple of days. The semi-darkness made it seem cooler, so we didn't bother switching on the lights. The blinds were still open and there was enough light coming in from outside for us to see by. I stepped back from her for a moment, drinking in the sight of her. She looked even more like an angel, in the white dress. An angel...maybe that was exactly what a monster like me needed.

I pushed her up against the wall of the hallway, knocking a picture off the wall. I slid my fingers through her hair, tangling them in it. My tongue traced the line of her upper lip and I kissed her, finding her open-mouthed and panting. I put a hand on her forehead, gently pinning her head for a second while I devoured her lower lip, nibbling and sucking. I thrust my other hand up the side of her dress, pushing the hem higher as it slid up her leg. God, her skin was so smooth, so perfect. I could feel her ass grinding against the wall in anticipation. I dodged past her bruised hip and started to rub her inner thigh in slow circles, toying with the edge of her panties. She gave a low moan in her throat, her breathing hitching faster and faster.

I was pushed between her thighs, grinding the hard bulge of my cock against her, but it wasn't enough. I had to feel every part of her. I pulled her away from the wall and spun her around so that her ass was against my crotch, my length nestled right between those firm, rounded cheeks. I kept one hand on her hip, rubbing and rubbing, never quite moving onto her panties, teasing her. I slid the other hand under her dress, under her bra, cupping her naked breast. *God,* but that felt good. The smooth roll of the flesh against my palm, the scrape of the hardening nipple against my fingers as I squeezed and rubbed. Then the urgent stiffening of the little bud as she groaned and writhed harder against me.

I half-walked, half-dragged her through to the living room. We collided with a coffee table and a stack of books and papers crashed to the floor. Both of us were panting, now, gasping our excitement. It was different to what happened on the gym roof, different even to the night before, when I'd gone down on her at my place. I'd been unleashed. My demons had let go of me, or maybe I'd let go of them. I knew it wasn't final. I knew that, eventually, I was going to have to tell her. But for now, I was free.

Both hands still under her dress, I guided her to the table and then lifted her so that she was sitting on the edge, pushing aside the stuff that was there. A vase tipped over and there was a glug of spilling water. She was breathless and wide-eyed in the semi-darkness, wondering what I was going to do next. I slid both hands down and hiked the dress the rest of the way up to her waist, baring those long, elegant legs.

I opened her thighs, going slow to make sure I didn't hurt her hip. Then I stepped between her knees and cupped her through her panties.

Second best feeling in the world? The soft warmth of a pussy against your palm. I didn't even have to move. Just the slight movement of her own breathing was enough to rub her lips against my hand through the thin fabric. And as soon as that started, that slow rasp wasn't enough. She needed more, and she started subtly grinding against me to get it.

Best feeling in the world? A woman grinding herself against your palm, to show how much she wants you. I kissed her again, this time just using my lips to part hers and letting *her* kiss *me*. Her tongue slipped into my mouth immediately, eagerly seeking mine out. I began to rub her gently through her panties, the heel of my hand grinding against her clit with each stroke, and she moaned, the sound vibrating against my lips.

I pulled back a little, breaking the kiss, because I wanted to look at her. She was absolute perfection. Sitting there on the edge of the table, that silky white dress still halfway decent on top, but hiked up to her hips down below. Her legs wantonly spread. Her long, black hair silky but disheveled where I'd run my hands through it again and again. And those soft, pink lips parted in pleasure, her breath coming in quick little pants. She really could have been a fallen angel, seduced by the devil.

She reached for me, eyes still closed, focused on the feel of my hand between her thighs. She started to undo my shirt buttons, doing it by feel. It was the perfect opportunity to gaze at her uninterrupted. That gorgeous face, marred only temporarily by that bitch who'd fought her. I wouldn't care even if those marks had lasted forever. She was perfect to me, no matter what.

My shirt came open. She leaned forward to kiss my chest and that moved her pussy against my hand. Both of us groaned. Then the soft touch of her lips against my pec. I caught my breath. She started to work her way down. When she licked at my nipple, I let out a growl. My cock felt as if it was going to rip right through my jeans.

I leaned forward, my mouth right next to her ear. "Does that feel good?" I ran my thumb across her pussy, strumming across the lips. I could feel her wetness soaking through her panties, but I wanted to hear her say it.

"*Yesss!*"

"Tell me what you want." We hadn't really done the dirty talk thing since the rooftop, but now I wanted more and more of it. The sound of her voice, low and throaty with excitement, was the ultimate turn on.

"I want you to *not stop,*" she whispered, her breath hot against my spit-slick nipple. She ground even harder into my hand.

"Like this?" I sped up a little.

"Oh, God, like *that!*"

"You're wet. You're soaking wet, Sylvie. I bet if I—" I couldn't resist it any longer. I grabbed her panties with both hands and pulled them down around her knees, stepping back to give myself room. Then I speared two fingers up inside her, hard and fast. God, she was soaking, her inner walls hot and silken, almost dripping for me. She cried out and closed her thighs hard around my hand, trapping it there. I began to pump my fingers. "God, you're so wet. Do you want it?" I pushed up against her leg, letting her feel the bulge at my crotch. "You want *this?*"

"Ah—*Yes....*"

I pumped faster, loving the feel of her, my long fingers sliding deep into her secret places. "Where? In your bedroom? On the couch?" I thrust faster still. "Where do you want me to fuck you, Sylvie?"

"R—Right here," she gasped. "Right here on the table."

35

SYLVIE

He stiffened a little and I felt my cheeks flush. God, had I gotten carried away? Had that sounded really slutty? It was his fault, him and his damn Irish accent. I'd never been big on talking dirty before, but with his voice it was incredible. I looked up at him, expecting him to look shocked.

He didn't look shocked. He looked more turned on than I'd ever seen him.

He stopped touching my pussy for the first time in what felt like hours and, as the cool air of the room hit my lips, I really felt how sopping I was down there. Sitting on the table edge, legs slightly apart, panties halfway down my thighs, I'd never felt so...*wanton*. Or so turned on.

His hands slid through my hair and he kissed me again, slow but deep. I felt his hands slide down my neck and then into the top of my dress and then he was reaching around, undoing the zipper with an expert hand. I felt the top of it loosen around my chest and my heart started hammering. I was already basically naked below the waist so I don't know why it seemed like a big deal, but the feeling of being systematically stripped...I don't know, it threw a switch somewhere in my brain. He pushed the dress off my shoulders and I felt the silky fabric slither down around my waist. Then he was kissing down my neck, leaving a trail of fire all the way down to my collarbone, and my bra was pulling tight for a second. I caught my breath in anticipation.

There—the clasp came free and my bra loosened. His hands skimmed the straps off my arms and it fell onto my lap. My breasts ached and throbbed in the cool air of the apartment, begging for his touch, my nipples hardening as much from the feel of his gaze on them as from their sudden exposure. Then his hands were on them, squeezing them together and lifting them in slow circles so that the sensitive flesh rubbed against his palms. He kissed all around my open, panting mouth: my cheeks, my chin, my upper lip, always leaving my mouth itself alone so that I could moan out loud.

Then his mouth was on my breasts, his tongue lapping at my nipples and swirling around them. He was just the right mixture of smooth and deliciously rough. First he'd kiss and lick at me, working his way inward across the breast to my nipple. Then he'd swirl his tongue around it in spirals, drawing it up to a quivering peak. And finally he'd bite gently at me, using his own lips as cushions over his teeth, until my feet were twisting together in circles and my nails were digging into the table top.

And then he'd do it all over again. It went on and on, lifting me closer and closer to my peak.

By the time he stopped, my breasts were shining and my hands were buried in that thick, dark Irish hair, dragging his head to me. I was trembling from being on the brink of an orgasm for so long. When he stepped back, I just sat there staring up at him, incapable of speech.

"I want you to come," he growled. "But I want to be in you. I want to feel it."

Oh Jesus yes!

He drew my panties down my legs and off, then tossed them away. He stepped between my legs, knocking them apart a little farther with his hips. Then he undid his belt and let his jeans slide down. The shape of him was clear through his jockey shorts and, a second later, it was there in his hand, thick and long and pointing right up between my spread thighs. He stared right at me as he took a condom from his pocket and rolled it on. I stared down at myself as he came closer and closer, watching the tip of him approaching me. I wasn't used to being able to see it like this, to actually watch as he—*Oh God!* The head of him pushed between my folds, spreading them. I felt myself opened up. It was different, like this, everything felt—*Ah!* He slid inside me, the girth of him stretching me just a little, making me grab for his shoulders. Everything felt different. And goddamn *great.*

He stepped closer, pushing right up against me as he slid deeper. It would have been awkward if I hadn't been so thoroughly, shamefully soaking for him. I let out a long moan and clasped my arms around his back as he pushed all the way into me, filling me completely. I squeezed my legs shut against his hips and that changed things again, making both of us gasp.

"I love fucking you," he said. "When I'm not with you, I dream about fucking you."

My brain and my heart did somersaults.

His hands went out to grip my hips...but at the last moment, he must have remembered my bruised hip because he grabbed my waist instead. He held me in place as he started to thrust, slowly at first but getting faster, those thickly-muscled thighs and tight ass giving him the power to really go at me. I threw my head back and luxuriated in the feel of him up inside me, so big, so gloriously wide, stroking against me, angled up so that he hit me in just the right spot—*God!*

Ribbons of hot pleasure were starting to swirl their way upward, spreading out to every part of me, flaring into fire when they touched my breasts or lips, anywhere he'd touched me. I started to jerk my hips towards him, wanting more of him. The table began to shake as we slammed our bodies together as hard as we damn well could. My hands came down to clutch at his ass, digging my fingers into the solid muscle there.

He sped up again and suddenly he lifted me and thrust his hands under my ass, cupping my cheeks. I groaned as he began to squeeze and knead me there in time with his thrusts. I'd been rocking back and forth a little before, but now his hands formed a firm little seat at the edge of the table, holding me in place for him. I groaned low in my throat as the increased friction sent me wild. Every thrust ended with a grind of his groin against my clit and I could feel the pleasure drawing tight, bursting free—

I came, eyes squeezed shut, legs and arms wrapped around him, shuddering helplessly against him. *His.* He groaned as my body squeezed at his cock, but I didn't feel him come.

When I regained my senses, he was moving very gently inside me. "Are you ready for more?" he asked in a low, utterly filthy voice.

More? I was still panting. But *hell yeah* I wanted more. I nodded.

He lifted me up to standing. And then turned me around to face the table. He pushed me up against it so that my groin was at the edge and then pushed gently on my back.

I got the idea, and the thought of it made a dark depth-charge of heat sink down to my groin and detonate there.

"Open your legs," he said. I'd never heard his voice so thick with lust.

I stepped my legs apart. I was still wearing my heels and that meant my ass was higher than the table top. If I wanted to put my chest down on the surface, I had to arch my back like a cat and tilt my pelvis...which of course, from where he was standing, was pretty much offering myself up to him. Again, I felt the heat of his gaze, this time licking down over my lower back and ass, eating me up. "Christ, Sylvie," he muttered. "You're incredible."

I'd turned my head to the side and was breathing a little fast. There was something about this position that made me—not nervous, exactly, but sort of weak and heady. Something about not being able to see him, about having this big, powerful man right between my spread thighs, with no warning of when he was going to—

Ah! The silken press of him against my lips, pushing me *in,* and then me opening to him and the hot surge of him right up into me. I let out a high little cry as he went deeper than before, deeper than he'd been up on the roof. *God!* I felt the slap of his balls against me, the press of the thick base of him against my lips, and I realized he was completely buried in me, as deep as a man can be. Instead of pulling back, he stayed there for a second, grinding in slow circles, and it felt amazing. He leaned right over me and bit the back of my neck, just barely nipping the skin with his teeth. I shuddered and moaned.

"I've been thinking about this," he said, "since that time you bent over the ropes in the ring."

I flushed, remembering it. *Me too.*

He kissed down my spine, as low as he could reach. Then he took hold of my ass and began to thrust. Almost immediately, I was rocketing up towards another orgasm. The way I was tilted up to meet him meant that, while my ass was in the air, my clit was rocking against the edge of the table. And he could go even harder and faster like this. He began to grunt as he pounded me and I threw my arms out over my head and grabbed for the far edge of the table. I knocked something heavy—a coffee mug, maybe—and it went spinning off the table and I heard it shatter. Then I was clutching, white-knuckled, to the wood. The orgasm was expanding inside me, filling me up, ready to burst. I had my eyes closed but, even if I'd opened them, I wouldn't have been able to see him. I was bent over and being ravished by some faceless stranger and it was filthy and raw and utterly hot, but at the same time safe. Because I knew it was him, and I knew he'd never hurt me.

"God," I gasped. "I'm going to. Going—to—"

"Go on," he said, his voice a low rasp. "Come for me, Sylvie. Be mine."

That pushed me over the edge. I threw my head back and groaned and cursed, pushing myself up with my hands and arching my back like a bow, and his lips found mine and we kissed as he shot and shot inside me and I shuddered around him.

36

AEDAN

I woke up with a start and then listened. *What was that? What the hell was that?!*

It took me several seconds to realize that the thing I could hear was *quiet*. No trucks. No clatter of chains and whir of cranes.

I wasn't in my apartment near the docks. I'd done what I never did: stayed over at some woman's place after sex.

And then my brain caught up. *Sylvie.* It wasn't some woman I'd picked up in a bar. It was my angel, and we were finally together. A warm calm descended on me. I smiled in the darkness.

I rolled over as carefully as I could. There she was—sound asleep, her black hair fanned out across the pillow. Her lips were slightly parted and she looked utterly serene. I could only see her bare shoulder, but I remembered her peeling off her dress before we fell into bed, which meant she was naked under the sheets. If I just pulled them back, I'd see every gorgeous inch of her....

I got up before I could succumb to temptation. I was wide awake and buzzing with energy, even though it was still the middle of the night. Why? Why wasn't I cuddled up with Sylvie, in the same deep sleep? God knows we'd fucked hard enough to be exhausted.

I found my shorts and pulled them on, then stumbled to the

bathroom. It was only when I turned on the light that I saw it. Something was different about me. I looked...*normal*. I looked like a boyfriend. Some guy that Sylvie had met at a coffee shop or on the subway. A nice, normal guy who could take her on dates and buy her presents. Someone, somewhere, had granted me my secret wish—

I was still half asleep, so it took me a few seconds to realize what had happened. In my bathroom, the light comes from the other side.

I twisted slightly and my scars appeared from the shadows that had been hiding them. And everything they represented slammed back into my mind.

Coming here hadn't fixed me at all. I hadn't changed. I'd just forgotten what I was for a few hours, thanks to lust...and maybe deeper feelings.

I'd been weak. I'd thought with my cock instead of putting her first. She said she wanted a bad boy but I was a *feck* of a lot more than a walk on the wild side. I was the worst sort of guy. She just didn't know it, yet.

For her sake, I had to push her away.

37

SYLVIE

In the shower the next morning, I looked down at my body. The changes were easy to see. My core had tightened up. My thighs and calves were toned from all the footwork. My posture had even gotten better, because I'd strengthened all the muscles in my back. And the bruises were fading a little, enough that they could be mostly covered with make-up.

When I came out, Aedan was making coffee, which made me want to kiss him. So I did, snuggling up behind him wearing only a towel and touching my lips to the back of his neck.

He tensed up. "Hi," he said.

I froze. Something was wrong. Something had changed, since we went to bed. He was back to that silent, brooding guy he'd been when I first met him. "What's up?"

"Nothing's up." He smiled, but it didn't reach his eyes. "Here. Coffee."

I frowned. "Aedan, what's the matter?"

"Nothing's the matter. Come on, let's go shopping."

Shopping? Neither of us had money for shopping. Was he going to surprise me again with another dress? That was sweet, but I couldn't let him do it a second time.

Or was this him attempting to be romantic? I suddenly relaxed. *That* was it! He was just some big, dumb guy and he was trying to play the boyfriend and getting it slightly wrong. Okay, I could live with that. It was actually kind of cute.

Something about it still didn't seem right, but I was ready to believe anything rather than admit something was horribly wrong.

I dressed and we headed out. When we hit the street, I wished I'd brought a jacket because the summer heat had finally built to the point where a storm felt inevitable. Already, dark clouds were spreading over the city, coming our way. But it was too late now.

On the subway, I tentatively took Aedan's hand and he smiled and held hands with me, but it felt mechanical and forced. Was this his past again, his belief that he shouldn't be with me? Or was it simpler than that—was this just morning-after regrets? Had he just wanted to fuck me and now he was looking for a way out? But then why not just say something at the apartment? What was the shopping trip all about?

It's romantic, I told myself furiously all the way to the mall. *It's romantic. What other reason could there be?* I just had to give him a chance. He hadn't dated in a long time so he wasn't used to all this hanging-out-together stuff. That's what it was.

And I wanted it to work so badly. He'd put on this faded blue t-shirt that hugged his arms and brought out his eyes and, every time I looked at him walking alongside me, my heart soared. This went beyond liking him, now. This was much more than that. *But what if he doesn't feel the same way?*

Of course he does. It's romantic. We walked into the mall. *It's a romantic shopping trip. In a minute, he's going to surprise you with—*

"Okay," he said, stopping and turning to me. "This'll do."

We'd stopped in the middle of the mall's main hall. My heart was pounding against my ribs, my face flushed with excitement. *I was right! What is it? What is it?*

"I want you," he said, "to start a fight."

His words rang around my head for a few seconds.

"What?" I croaked.

He crossed his arms, which meant he had to let go of my hand. I looked down stupidly at my empty palm. "You were intimidated by Jacki," he told me. "A fight's not just about fists. Half of it's in the mind. You've got to get up in her face, next time. You've got to let her know she's going to lose. Once she believes that, she *will* lose." He looked around us. "So pick a woman and start something."

"Wh—What?" Someone had driven a chisel into my chest and was hammering it home, cracking me apart. I felt so goddamn stupid. Of course it had just been about sex. Of course this wasn't some big romantic gesture. It was a training exercise. But I couldn't let him see how upset I was. I felt stupid enough as it was. I redirected my pain. "I can't just attack someone!" I snapped.

"You don't have to hit her. Just get in her face. Yell at her."

"I can't do that!" My voice was savage and raw, all of the hurt spilling out. "I'm not some psycho!"

I stared at him. He didn't answer but he knew. I could see it in his eyes. He knew he was hurting me and he didn't want to. *So why are you doing it? Why are you playing games with me?*

And then I remembered how I'd pressed him the night before, outside the restaurant. He'd told me he shouldn't be with me, that he was wrong for me, and I'd kept right on pushing. Was this the inevitable outcome? The sex was done, and now we had to go back to being just pupil and mentor? For the first time in a long while, Alec's warning swam back into my brain.

What if the stuff in Aedan's past was bad? *Really* bad? What if Alec had been right all along? What if this whole thing really had been doomed from the start and I was the only one too stupid not to see it?

No. I couldn't accept that.

I shook my head determinedly. "I can't just yell at some woman. I don't even know these people. I don't hate them. I can't just turn it on like that."

He put a hand on my shoulder. Despite everything, it felt good.

"Do you hate Jacki?" he asked.

I hadn't ever thought about it. I was scared of her—scared as hell.

And angry, because she'd hit me and humiliated me. But she'd done all that because Rick had ordered her to. She probably needed the money just as badly as Alec and I did. "No," I said at last.

"You've *got* to be able to turn it on," he said gently. "You've got to be able to *hate* your opponent. You've got to want to destroy her. You've got to think that you *deserve* to win. She has to be scared of you. That's the only way this works."

I shook my head again. "I don't know how to do that."

"That's why you're going to learn. Go on."

I stood there and stared at him. I didn't say anything, but my eyes were pleading with him. *Tell me! Tell me what's going on! What's changed?*

I saw his eyes soften slightly. He didn't want this any more than I did. But at the same time, he wasn't going to change his mind. He was back to being my trainer—what I needed, not what I wanted. "Go on," he said firmly.

I turned and walked away. I could feel the tears prickling at my eyes, but I blinked them back. God, I was pathetic. I was crying, just as I needed to be intimidating and strong. Because the worst part was, I knew Aedan was right. I *did* need to learn this stuff, or I'd be continually backing away from Jacki next time I met her, hitting the wall and tripping over my own feet in my hurry to get away.

I tried to think of what Aedan would do.

Aedan would *man the fuck up.*

I looked around for a woman on her own, because that seemed like a good place to start. I felt worryingly like a lion, looking for the weak deer to prey on. Someone who'd scare easily.

But each time I headed towards someone, I veered away at the last moment. That fifty-something woman with the fussy neck scarf? That was someone's grandmother. The harassed mom towing a three year-old? I couldn't yell at her—the kid would hear.

And then I nearly ran right into someone. Bleached blonde hair and a smile that was all lip gloss and confidence. About my age, but socially the polar opposite. Her arms were loaded down with bags and she was flanked on either side by what I thought of as bookend friends—designed to support her and make her look good. One had glossy black hair, one chestnut. They only needed a redhead and they'd have a complete set.

The leader didn't say anything. She just looked at my cheap t-shirt and my worn jeans and sneakers and her lips curled into a patronizing, fake-apologetic sneer. She exchanged a quick look with her friends, as if to say, *Oh dear.*

I stumbled back a few paces to get out of their way, but not fast enough. The blonde tossed her hair and they walked around me. It wasn't anything that hadn't happened a million times before, on the street or in a bar. It was just how it worked, how the social elite let everyone else know who was in charge.

I thought of how scared I'd been of Jacki. How scared I'd been of everyone, my whole life.

And I reached out and grabbed one of the blonde's shopping bags.

She pulled up short as the handle snapped tight. "Hey!" She rounded on me. "What the fuck?"

For the first time in my life, I took a step forward, towards the danger. "Why don't you watch where you're going, bitch?" My voice didn't sound how I wanted it to sound at all. It was a thin, shaky croak.

There was a second's silence and then she burst out laughing, close enough to my face that I could feel her warm spit hit me. Her breath smelled of cherry lip gloss. Her friends joined in.

I drew myself up to my full height. My fear was still there but a hot tide of anger was overwhelming it. "Why don't you watch where you're going—*bitch?*" I said again. And this time, my voice didn't shake at all.

She stopped laughing. Her eyes betrayed just the tiniest flicker of fear, like a crack in the side of a mountain. But a crack was all I needed to split that smug exterior wide open, if I muscled my way into it. "I'm not scared of you," she said.

"Yes you fucking are."

She glanced sideways at her friends, who'd stopped laughing.

"You think they're going to help you?" I asked, my voice low and cold, now. I nodded to the store we were standing next to. "You think they're going to stop me when I push your goddamn face through that window?"

She went pale.

I leaned in close. "Say sorry," I said.

Her mouth moved a few times, trying to form some snarky put-down, but she couldn't quite get it out. Our faces were close enough to kiss, her eyes huge and terrified. "Sorry," she whispered at last.

I let go of her bag and leaned back. She gathered her friends and ran. People around us were looking at the scene in horror and then quickly walking away as soon as I turned in their direction.

Aedan's hand landed on my shoulder. "Well done," he said sincerely.

I looked at his hand. All I wanted to do was to put my own hand on top of it, and then turn around and kiss him. But I knew, instinctively, that wasn't on the table. Something had happened, since last night. Something had changed to slingshot us back to how we used to be, before the rooftop. If I pushed him now, I might lose him completely.

"You want to get some breakfast?" he asked.

I nodded sadly.

Breakfast, in a shopping mall food court, might mean bagels or pastries or muffins. Except when you're a boxer and you need *protein, protein, protein.*

I eyed my burger. It was ten in the morning. "The whole thing?" I asked.

"You can leave the bun, if you want." He passed me a carton of milk.

As we ate, I went through about a thousand different things I could say. And none of them felt like they'd work. I couldn't believe that this sudden coldness was because he was looking for a way out now that we'd had sex a couple of times. Not Aedan. He was better than that. So it had to be his past, again.

Last time, I'd pushed him. I wasn't going to make the same mistake again. So I sat there and ate and talked strategy and how we'd focus on keeping my guard up and pushing forward instead of falling back. And the whole time, all I wanted to do was to lean across the table and kiss him.

That was why I was distracted when I went to empty my tray. I didn't see the guy coming until he was right up behind me. When I turned around, he was practically touching me.

"Hi," he said to my chest.

He was a cocky confident son of a bitch, with close-cropped blond hair and a t-shirt that showed off his muscles. He was right in my personal space. I sidestepped, but he moved with me, chuckling as if it was all a big joke.

"What's your name?" he asked.

I wanted to say *I'm not interested* or *No thanks* or maybe just *Fuck off*, but none of them would come out. He was too big and too male. I wasn't sure what he'd do if I pissed him off. So I just shook my head.

"You don't have a name?" he asked, as if that was the best joke in the world.

I didn't know where to look. My eyes were everywhere except on his face, because I didn't dare provoke him by making eye contact.

He moved in even closer. Close enough that his chest touched my nipples. Just a brush, as if it was accidental, but I saw the smile that said it wasn't. We were right up against each other, now. We would have looked like lovers, if I hadn't looked so petrified. *Stop this! Can't you see I'm not enjoying this?* But he didn't notice. Or didn't care.

"She wants you to leave her alone." An Irish voice, from just outside my field of view.

The guy barely looked up. "Fuck off."

I heard the brutal smack of a punch landing and he flew sideways, tumbling six or seven feet through the air before he smashed into a table and chairs, scattering them like bowling pins. People screamed and jumped to their feet. I stared aghast at Aedan as he lowered his fist. I'd forgotten what happened when he hit someone. Behind the counter, I could see the burger store owner talking frantically into his radio.

"Come on," I said. "Quick!" And I dragged him out of the food court and towards the exit of the mall. I wanted to hug him for saving me but he looked sullen...almost angry. Why would he be angry at *me?*

Outside, the storm had finally broken and rain was pelting down —the hard, unforgiving kind that soaks you to the skin in about five seconds flat. Everyone else was huddled inside the doors, waiting for it to pass, but I knew mall security would catch up with us any second. I pulled Aedan outside, into the rain, and ran down the street.

The rain plastered our t-shirts to our bodies. By the time we reached the end of the street, our jeans were soaked through and shining. The rain was coming down fast enough that the sidewalks were awash.

I pulled Aedan into an alley, looking for shelter. At least the rain would put the mall cops off chasing us. We stopped beside some dumpsters. It hit me that I wasn't out of breath, despite running half a block. All those early-morning runs had paid off.

I looked around for something to hide under, but there was nothing. Besides, we were already as wet as we could possibly be. It would almost have been funny, if it hadn't been for the tension that had been building all morning, and Aedan's sour expression. "*What?*" I yelled, finally cracking. "Why are you angry with me?"

He stared at me. "You should have hit that guy. You should have stood up for yourself."

I looked at him incredulously. "*What?*"

He looked even madder. "He was touching you! You know how to get in someone's face, now. Why didn't you?"

"You think it was *my fault?!* Jesus, are you going to start blaming rape victims next?"

"What are you talking about? I just want you to be able to stand up for yourself!" His eyes were flashing with anger, but I could see the concern there, too. "You did it with the woman at the mall. Why not him?"

Oh. My. God. "You *cannot* be that stupid! *He was a guy!*"

"So what?"

"Are you *kidding me?!* Because—Because—" I stood there, rain streaming down my face, trying to find the words. "Because he's a *man!* Because I'm a woman! Don't you—don't you get it?"

He stood there staring at me.

"Don't you get what we're scared of, when we get into any kind of a fight with a man?"

I saw realization finally dawn. But he shook his head. "No," he said. "Not all men."

"*Yes!* All fucking men! When it's a stranger, and he's right in your face and he's being aggressive! Jesus, how could you not know that?" My hair was being plastered across my face by the rain. I pushed it angrily out of the way. "You've taught me to fight; I'm still a woman!"

His hands were bunching into fists, now. He didn't want it to be true. "Not most guys. Some guys, maybe. Not most of us."

The rain had chilled me to the bone, now, and I was shivering. "Not all the time. But when you're a woman and a guy's aggressive with you—yes! We always have that fear!"

He stared at me for a long time and I could see it slowly sinking in. "Jesus," he said at last. Then, "Even me?"

I shook my head, some of the anger leaving me. "No. Not you. I've never felt that way about you."

He nodded slowly and then turned away. "I'm sorry," he said at last. "I'm really sorry. I just..." He shook his head in frustration and punched the dumpster so hard it rocked on its wheels. "I love you and I just want to protect you!"

The rain hissed down between us, a solid wall of water. "What?" I said, my voice breaking.

He shook his head. "I can't—"

"Yes! Yes, you can! Aedan, I love you too! I just—I don't know what's going on with us! Talk to me! Tell me why you keep pushing me away!"

He shook his head again, glancing towards the street. I knew he was seconds away from walking off into the rain and, if he did, I wasn't sure I'd ever see him again. "Tell me! What can be so bad? Come on, if you really love me then talk to me!"

He stared at the ground for a moment, the rain sluicing down his face. Then he finally looked up at me and nodded.

38

AEDAN

"I'd just come over from Ireland," I said. "Things had gone to hell with my family—that's a whole different story—so I was pretty much on my own. But I was cocky as hell. I'd won those local championships back home and I thought I was going to be the next big thing. But I didn't have a manager. No one knew me, no one wanted to take me on. I wound up at the bottom of the barrel."

"The Pit," Sylvie said slowly. "With Rick."

I nodded. "I needed the money and it didn't seem so bad, at first. I won my first five fights and that was a big deal, in that place. I was the champ and even in a shitty place like that, that means something. But the problem was, the better I got, the more people wanted to take me on."

She nodded. I could see her tensing up, preparing herself.

"There's only ever been two things I'm good at: fighting and fucking. I feel...*right* when I'm in the ring. Like that's where I'm supposed to be." I sighed. "I told you: I'm just a thug."

She shook her head defiantly. So I continued.

"Rick keeps putting me up against people. Some of them start coming in from out of town, and people are betting big money and Rick, he's taking his cut from the bookies. 'Course, *I* don't see much of it, but I'm doing okay. And Rick's always telling me, '*You're my boy. You're the best at this. You were made to do this.*' But then Rick starts wanting me to do stuff outside the ring. He wants me to accompany him around town."

"Like a bodyguard?"

I shook my head bitterly. "Like a feckin' dog. A weapon he can use to scare people. I don't want to do it but I'm young and naive...I tell myself it's not so bad. I mean, I'm just there for show. I'm not going to *do* anything. And it works, for a while. People who owe him money pay up. People invading his turf get the hell out. Everyone's happy— except me. And Rick keeps telling me, '*You're my attack dog. You growl when I tell you to growl. Just a big, dumb, snapping hound.*' And I start to believe him."

I swallowed slowly. "But then, one day, it stops working. Some storeowner owes Rick money and won't pay. So he has me smash their store." I gave Sylvie a sickly grin. "You know how good I am at smashing stuff. And as I'm tearing up the place, I'm telling myself it's okay because it's only stuff—it's not people. And Rick's still telling me how good I am at this shit, how it's a good job he's here to make use of me, because no one else would want a stupid thug like me. And I guess I start to believe that, too."

Sylvie had gone pale. I'd known all along that this would happen. I'd known that, once she found out what I really was, her whole view of me would change. But I was too deep into this to stop now.

"Then, a few weeks later, some guy disrespects Rick. So Rick tells me to break his arm." I stared at the wall, unable to meet her eyes. "And the crazy thing is, as I'm feeling the bones snap, I'm telling myself *it's only an arm. He'll recover.* As if that makes it okay." And Rick keeps telling me, '*This is all you're good for—beating seven shades of shit out of people.*' I took a deep breath. "And so it went on. Each week, I'd pummel some guy in the ring. The other days, I'd beat up whoever Rick told me to. Eventually, it all sort of blended together. I'd fight and then I'd come home and wash the blood off and go find some woman to fuck to help me forget. Rick's happy and I'm making money. But when I look in the mirror, I don't even recognize myself."

I felt suddenly very tired. I slumped against the dumpster and slid down it until I was sitting on the soaked ground. Sylvie suddenly knelt and threw her arms around me. She didn't say anything. She just held me. I think she sensed that the worst was still to come.

"This is where you think I saw the light," I said bitterly. "This is where you think I had a revelation and turned around and stuck it to Rick." I shook my head. "But that's not what happened." I took a deep breath. "See, Rick had a problem. I was at my peak—every fight, I was getting better. I started getting calls from people who thought I could make it on the proper circuit. Rick figured it was only a matter of weeks until someone stole me away. So he came up with a plan."

"He put me up against this guy called Travere. Eric Travere. I'd fought him before a few times—a Frenchman, living in New York. Pretty good—a brawler, like me, but with a better reach. Killer left hook. But normally, I could have taken him. He could dish it out, but he couldn't take it. A few good hits, maybe a couple of rounds, and he'd go down."

Sylvie took my hand, and I realized I've made fists. I tried to force myself to relax, but I couldn't.

"I get in the ring and, right away, I know something's wrong. There's a look in Eric's eyes, like he's going to win *no matter what.* We go for it and he starts slamming that left hook into me. I hit him a few times and he staggers, but he stays on his feet. Second round comes and it's the same thing. I'm hitting him but he's just not going down. Third round and the crowd are going nuts—they've never seen anyone last this long against me. And Rick, he's there in that side room, grinning away and I *know* something's wrong."

I let the rain wash down my face for a moment, but it didn't make me feel any cleaner. I swallowed, feeling the nausea rising in my throat. "Fourth round. The guy's bleeding from his head and I'm pretty sure I've broken some ribs. I get him in a clinch and I scream at him over the crowd"—my voice broke and it took a second before I could continue—"*'Go down, you moron! What the feck is the matter with you? Go down!'* But he stays on his feet. Fifth round and he's staggering—he just doesn't have the energy to continue. So"—I swallowed and looked down at my lap for a second, then back to Sylvie—"so he grabs a broken bottle—back then, Rick didn't used to have anyone sweep up before a fight. And he runs at me and, before I know what's happening, he shoves it into my neck—"

Sylvie clapped a hand over her mouth, going pale.

"The blood starts gushing between my fingers and he's still stabbing and twisting and I know that any second, he's going to cut the vein and then I'm dead. I try to get it out of his hand, but he's hanging onto that bottle for dear life. And I can see it in his eyes: he's going to finish me. He's *that* desperate to win—he's just going to go until I'm dead." I swallowed. "So I grab his shirt and pull him off his feet and down to the ground, and I start punching his face, because it's the only way I can see to make him stop, and his head's bouncing off the concrete and, after four punches, he lets go of the bottle. And he's dead."

Sylvie sat there in shock for a moment. I knew what she was going to say: that it was self defense, that I had no choice.

"That's not the end of the story," I told her. The words were hard to get out, now, each one foul and bitter. "The crowd ran. I sat there against the wall with my hand on my neck, blood dripping out of me, just staring at the body. Eventually, Rick's goons show up and get rid of it. I wad up a towel and manage to stop the bleeding and stumble off to a doctor I know—someone who does stuff off the books. She tells me the guy missed my jugular by a hair. Really, I need a plastic surgeon to fix all the damage, but I can't go near a hospital or there'll be questions. She does the best she can with sutures, but I'm pretty much a patchwork by the end of it and it heals badly." I ran my hand over the thick, ugly scars. "Hence the mess."

Sylvie nodded, tears in her eyes.

"Everything goes quiet for a few days. Some rumors go around that someone's been killed and the cops sniff about, but no one's talking. Rick's pretty good at this stuff—no one ever finds Travere's body so, eventually, the cops drop it. I'm still in shock, but I figure I've been lucky. And I figure that I had no choice. He was some crazy fighter who went too far."

I took a deep breath. "Then I found out...he had a wife. And two kids. He was pretty much done with fighting, close to quitting until I came along and became the champ." I shook my head. "See, Rick knew I was going to leave, sooner or later. So he needed to make as much money out of me as he could. He finds Travere—a guy who everyone knows I can beat. But he puts his own bet on —*against* me. And he takes Travere's little girl and tells him that he'll never see her again unless he kills me in the pit. Travere didn't want to kill me. He was just doing what he had to, to protect his family."

"It's not your fault," Sylvie told me. "Rick used you. He set you up."

I shook my head. "It should have been me who died. He had a wife and kids. I had feckin' no one. He had a life, outside of fighting. I was just a thug." I looked into her eyes. "Tell me the world wouldn't be a better place if I'd bled out, and that guy had gone home to his family that night."

Sylvie's mouth moved a few times, but she couldn't find the words.

"Afterwards, I guess Rick didn't know what the feck to do. He must have been mad as hell at losing his money, but he also must have figured I'd want to kill him. So I stayed clear of him and he didn't come after me. I thought about turning myself in to the cops. The only thing that stopped me was the family. Rick gave the kid back the same night—she wasn't hurt or anything. But he knew where they lived. If I copped to the murder, Rick would go down as an accessory, and he'd kill the mother to stop her testifying about any of it."

"So I quit. I got the first job I could, down at the docks, and moved into that shitty apartment, and decided I'd never fight again. But that didn't fix anything. The first time I took the bandages off and saw my neck, I smashed the mirror. I realized what I'd become." I turned to Sylvie. "It wasn't just killing Travere in the ring. It was all the stuff I did for Rick. All those people I hurt. That's all I'm good for, Sylvie— breaking stuff and causing pain. And *I don't want that for you.*"

I looked at her and I prayed. I prayed that I was wrong. I prayed that she'd say something to make it okay.

But she just stared at me in horror and I knew I'd been right all along. I was exactly the monster I thought I was.

I got up and walked away.

39

SYLVIE

Say something.

He was a killer. He'd actually killed someone and hurt many more.

Stop him.

Every warning my dad had ever given me ran through my head. Every concept of *bad men*. Ex-cons, with their prison tattoos. Rick's bodyguards. Men I'd cross the street to avoid. Most of those men hadn't killed anyone. But Aedan had.

Call him back right now or you're going to lose him.

I tried to find a way around it. *It was self-defense. He had no choice.* But I couldn't get past the image of the guy lying there on the floor of the pit, or his wife and kids at home. The knowledge was like a rock, crushing me down into the ground. This man I...*loved*...was a killer. Those same hands that had touched every part of my body had —*Jesus.*

I watched him disappear around the corner and then just sat there, head hunched against the rain. I let it soak through my hair and stream to the ground. I let it run down inside my t-shirt and flow down my back.

I imagined Rick slapping Aedan's back after each fight, telling him over and over again how vicious he was. In some ways, it was a dark version of what Aedan had done for me—he'd changed his whole view of himself. But where Aedan had convinced me I could be strong, Rick had convinced Aedan that he was good for nothing but fighting. He'd twisted his mind. He was like a cruel dog owner who whips his animal until it snaps at anyone who comes near.

And Aedan had finally broken free of all that and sentenced himself to a life of solitude. And I'd showed up and asked him to train me...to *hit* me. God, that must have been unbearable for him. Just agreeing to train me, going back to that whole world...I felt sick at what I'd put him through. And yet he'd done it all, and for a stranger. I thought back to when he'd gone to The Pit with me and volunteered to take my place. He'd actually been willing to return to fighting—his worst nightmare—and for Rick, a man he must hate more than anyone in the world. All to protect me.

Maybe he was right—there was no fixing this. Nothing would bring back the man he'd killed. But he was trying to redeem himself. Shouldn't that count for something?

I sat there frozen for another few seconds...and then jumped to my feet and raced after him.

Out on the street, out of the shelter of the alley, the rain pounded at your head and flooded your eyes. Cars had slowed down to a crawl and were sending huge fantails of rainwater up onto the sidewalk. I had to squint just to see Aedan—he was almost half a block away and moving fast.

"Aedan!" I yelled. No response.

I started to run. Rain was streaming down my face and getting in my mouth, making it difficult to breathe. I tried to go faster, but my sneakers were sodden sponges and my soaked jeans weighed me down. At every side street I had to double-check for trucks pulling out, because the rain made it impossible to hear. "*Aedan!*"

I never could have caught him if I hadn't gotten into shape. But slowly, agonizingly, I gained. I was panting and gasping when I finally caught his arm and spun him around. Every muscle in his body was tense. He stared down at me, braced and ready. Ready for whatever useless platitude I could offer. Ready for me to lie and say it was okay. I knew none of that was going to work.

"You fucked up," I said at last, spitting it out through the rain. "You did a really bad thing. But you're already paying for it, every day. I've seen the way you look at yourself. Walking away from this, walking away from *me*—that's not making things better. Torturing yourself won't help."

"You really want to be around someone like me?"

"*Yes!*" I took his face between my hands. "Rick used you! He manipulated you *and* Eric. He's the one who should suffer." I gently put my arms around him. "I can't make this go away—ever. I can't even tell you it's okay, or that you shouldn't feel guilty. But I can tell you I love you."

He stared at me. Those pale blue eyes were burning brighter than I'd ever seen them, *wanting* it to be true.

So I showed him the only way I could. I threw myself at him and kissed him. For a split second, his lips stayed closed. And then I felt his body relax against mine as the guilt bled out. I'd felt the weight of the knowledge for just a few seconds, back in the alley, and it had been unbearable. He'd been carrying that weight for years...and now it had finally been lifted.

We pulled each other closer, wrapping warm arms around rain-chilled waists. My breasts crushed against his chest and I could feel the beat of his heart through the sodden layers of our t-shirts. He lifted me off the ground and I clung to him, wrapping my legs around his waist. The rain poured down our faces, but it couldn't hold back the heat of the kiss as we gasped and panted and his tongue explored my mouth. The heat of him warmed my chilled body, sending shudders out to my fingertips. At first, it was about reassurance—letting each other know that we were *back*, that it was going to be okay. But slowly, it changed, becoming hotter and deeper. I could feel all the barriers between us finally lifting...leaving us free.

He drew back for a second, gazing at me as if to check he wasn't dreaming. "God," he rasped. "God, now I got you...I'm gonna do such bad things to you."

I was naive enough to think he meant *when we get home.*

He set me down, took my hand and dragged me towards the nearest structure—a parking garage. His warm, urgent grip and the way he squeezed my hand in excitement was exactly what I'd longed for that morning on the subway. Everything was different, now. We were properly together for the first time.

When we reached the garage, he didn't bother walking around to the entrance. He just lifted me over the low wall and inside, then vaulted the wall himself. The place was full of cars, but there didn't seem to be anyone around—a good thing, judging by the looks Aedan was giving me. I don't think he would have cared if there had been anyone around. At that point, I think he'd have happily fucked me in a police station.

I managed to steer him a little way away from the street, into the dark maze of cars, but he ran out of patience after just a few seconds and pushed me up against an SUV, his hands sliding up underneath my t-shirt. His lips found mine and his tongue slipped into my mouth. His hands cupped my breasts and he pinned me against the car, my wet shirt squeaking along the window. When the family who owned it came back for it that evening, they must have wondered why their car was dripping wet, indoors.

Then he stripped my t-shirt up and over my head.

"Not here," I gasped. "We can't."

"Yes we feckin' can."

He reached behind me for the clasp of my bra, but his fingers kept slipping on the wet fabric. Frustrated, he flipped me around and pushed me forward against the car. My breasts pillowed against the driver's side window, the glass shockingly cold. When he stripped off my bra and pulled me back against him, I saw my breasts had left a sideways figure of eight on the glass. Then his hands were cupping them, thumbs stroking across nipples that were already achingly hard.

He lifted me and set me down on my back on the hood of the SUV. I lay there staring up at him, panting. *We're not going to—God, we can't, not right here in public—*

He started to unfasten my belt. In the distance, I could hear voices. In the huge, echoey space, it was impossible to tell where they were coming from. They could be heading for this very car, for all I knew.

Aedan stripped my jeans, sneakers and socks off in one twisted wet bundle. A second later, my panties followed and I was naked on the hood. The metal must have been freezing under my ass, but I didn't even register it. All I cared about was the sight of the man in front of me as he slowly unfastened his belt and shucked down his jeans. He didn't bother taking off any more clothes. His cock was already fully hard for me and he took it in one hand as he stepped towards me. He looked right into my eyes, but I couldn't meet them— I couldn't stop looking at his cock as he nudged my knees apart and stepped between them.

I gasped as he pulled me to the very edge of the hood. He bent my knees up and back so that I was wide open to him. The heat was flooding through me, lashing and whipping around like a living thing. I grabbed my legs and held them there. He rolled on a condom and stepped closer, until the tip of his cock just split my folds, and I could feel how wet I was for him.

"I'm going to fuck you, Sylvie," he told me. "So hard."

I went weak.

He lunged into me and I cried out as his thickness spread me. With my legs up like that, he could go *deep,* and he did. He leaned right over me, his hands going to my waist and then sliding up my body to my breasts. My skin was icy cold from the rain but inside I was scalding hot, and every movement of him inside me pushed the heat further and further outward. My nipples rasped along his palms and the heat turned dark and oily inside me, a low groan escaping me.

He started to thrust, and I knew neither of us was going to last long. It was quiet in the garage and I could hear the wet slap of our bodies meeting and the low, hard sound of his breathing as he filled me again and again. For the first time, he was utterly free, with nothing holding him back. He pressed me down on the hood, his thumb and forefingers pinching lightly at my nipples, and slammed into me in hard, savage thrusts. I could feel the heat swirling and building, taking form. I started to cry out on each stroke, my eyes tight shut and my head thrashing against the hood.

Voices again, closer, this time. On our floor and heading towards us.

Aedan didn't stop. He leaned down and kissed me, muffling my cries with his mouth as he thrust and thrust.

The people must have been only a handful of rows away. I could hear them asking each other where they left the car.

His cock was silken perfection inside me, solid and hotly thick and wonderful. My climax built and built and I could feel Aedan getting close, too, his thrusts becoming faster but more erratic. I grabbed his shoulders and squealed in ecstasy, my cry muffled by his lips. "*MFFF!*"

The world suddenly exploded into noise—a howling banshee cry. I was too far gone to care, and so was Aedan. Three more thrusts and he thrust deep and held there, wrapping his arms around me, and I felt him shudder and shoot inside me in long bursts. I clung to his shoulders, arching my back as I came too, clenching and tightening around him.

"*Jesus!*" said a man's voice, right next to us.

I opened my eyes and looked up. Two businessmen were standing there staring at us. It was only then that I realized the SUV's alarm was going off.

Aedan pulled me off the hood and grabbed my clothes and we ran, staggering and giggling. And happy.

40

AEDAN

For the next two weeks, Sylvie trained like crazy. With the barriers between us removed, we could both focus on getting her ready to fight Jacki. Both of our futures hung on her winning. If she won, she'd be free...and I was starting to believe that maybe I'd redeem myself.

Telling Sylvie about my past had changed everything. Hitting things still felt good, as it always had, but now it felt honest and clean, not darkly addictive. I started to have daydreams about going back to fighting, when all of this was over. Not for some scumbag like Rick, but on the official amateur circuit. It was a crazy dream and I knew it...but at least I was daring to dream again.

We spent almost every waking hour together, at the gym or at my place. She basically moved in, disappearing only for her few remaining shifts at the hotel. I hated to think of her down on her knees, scrubbing for rich guests who barely acknowledged her. But she needed to keep a job. If she won, she needed a future after this.

If she won. She was getting better each day, not just at the basics of punching and footwork but at the little tricks. I taught her headbutts and elbows to the face, eye gouges and stamps to the back of the leg. Some of it would be useless when fighting a woman, of course, like the knee to the groin. But I figured she'd be able to hold her own against Jacki.

We got past our fear of hitting each other. We left the sparring for the end of the day, when the gym was deserted and the owner was dozing in his office with a dead six-pack of beer. Then we'd get in the ring and turn it into a game. We'd circle and pant, the adrenaline flooding our veins like a drug. I'd lose myself in the gleaming perfection of her sweat-slick skin, in those gorgeous green eyes, narrowed in concentration. I'd throw big, heavy punches at her, but she'd dart out of the way, gasping and sometimes giggling, letting fly with flurries of her own and sometimes landing one. And eventually, when the tension got too much, I'd rush her and pin her up against the corner post and snog her. And we'd stand there, tongues entwined, punching and kissing, before I finally dragged her off to the rooftop.

A few days before the fight, I figured she needed a break so I took her for a picnic in Central Park. Nothing fancy—just pastrami on rye and takeout coffees. But we sat in the sun, with Sylvie in a little strappy top, and *feck me* if we didn't look just like some real, happy couple who'd met through a dating site, or a matchmaking friend or something.

Connor's girlfriend, Karen, was playing as part of a string quartet —not really my kind of music, but it was relaxing. And there were some other girls from the same posh performing arts place— ballerinas, doing pirouettes and those spooky jump things, where it looks like they don't weigh anything at all. Sylvie was sitting between my legs on the grass. I wrapped my arms around her from behind, put my chin on her shoulder and pretended I wasn't watching the dancers too hard.

"You're looking at the ballet dancers, aren't you?" asked Sylvie.

"What ballet dancers?" I kissed her ear.

She twisted around and whispered. *"You could always buy me a leotard."* I felt my cock harden against her ass. Then, watching the dancers do the standing splits, she added, "Not sure I could manage *that,* though."

"I'd rather have you," I told her truthfully. The dancers were pretty and all, but they were nothing compared to Sylvie. I looked around at the people watching the dancers, because if Karen and Connor were here and their other friends were here—

Even as I thought it, a shadow fell across us—one with curves that reminded me of an old movie femme fatale. I looked up into a cloud of auburn hair.

"Your shopping trip worked out, then," said Jasmine.

I introduced them and, even if Sylvie was just a *little* suspicious at me knowing a TV star, they were chatting away happily within minutes. When Jasmine left, she gave me a sidelong glance and a grin that said, *You've done good. Don't mess it up.*

I grinned back at her, squeezed Sylvie a little tighter, and nodded. *I won't.*

41

SYLVIE

It was the day before the fight and the tension was starting to win out over my new-found happiness. "You think I can take her?" I asked for about the thirtieth time that day. We'd just come out of a lengthy session of bag work and my arms felt like limp noodles.

"You bloody better," Aedan told me. "I'll have money on you."

I gave him a one-two to the chest. "Be serious!"

"I am. I *will* have money on you."

I hit him again and then hugged him. After a few seconds, he stroked my hair and said, "Yeah. You'll beat her. You're stronger than her and faster than her and you've learned to fight dirty. You're ready."

I shook my head slowly. "I still can't believe...I'm going to have to hit her. I mean, *really* hit her, like knock her down so she can't get back up."

He squeezed me. "You'll be able to put her down, when the time comes. She's used to dishing it out, not taking it." He pulled back a little and looked deep into my eyes. "I know what you're worried about, but she'll be okay. And you only ever have to do this once."

I nodded, but I couldn't get rid of the tightness in my chest.

"You'll whup her ass," said Aedan in a very bad American accent.

"Stop! That's awful!"

"You'll open a can of whup-ass on her."

I started to laugh, despite the tension. "*Stop!* We don't talk like that!"

"Oh *hell yeah*—she better get her books ready, 'cos you're gonna take her to *school.*"

I kissed him to shut him up. "I'm going to take a shower," I told him, "and then stop at the store and pick up a few things for dinner. You coming?"

He glanced at the punchbag. I'd noticed him doing that a lot, recently, which was why I'd asked. "You mind if I stay here—just for half an hour?"

I grinned. "Sure. I'll see you at your place." He'd given me his spare key a week before. When he handed it to me and curled my fingers around it, my heart had felt as if it was going to launch off into space. I was about to face the scariest thing in my entire life, but I was happier than I had been in years. Maybe, just maybe, if I won against Jacki, I could get my life back. Not just the one I had before Alec was injured but a new one, a better one, one where I woke up every morning in Aedan's arms.

And Aedan was happier, too, since he'd opened up to me. I could see him looking at the gym and our training differently. He was thinking about going back to it. That's why I was ecstatic to see him wanting to thump the bag on his own for a while. Sure, he'd used to come to the gym before I met him, but that was to lift weights and work off stress. This was him getting back into his old life again, like shaking out an old uniform and discovering it still fits. Rick had convinced him that he was nothing more than a thug. Now, he was slowly returning to the guy who'd first come over from Ireland, the one who'd wanted to be a boxer, not a fighter. The idea of him fighting again, even on the official circuit, scared the hell out of me...but not as much as the idea of him never doing the thing he loved again.

I took a quick shower and practically bounced out onto the street. There was a pretty good grocery store almost next door and I bought bell peppers and ground beef, onions and spices. I figured I'd make a chili. When I came out, I was so preoccupied that I didn't even see the car pull up behind me, or the window wind down.

"Sylvie," said a voice I recognized.

I spun around. Rick was in the back seat of an aging but still impressive Rolls Royce. One of his bodyguards was driving and the other was riding shotgun.

"Get in," said Rick. "We're going for a little ride."

I glanced back at the gym. "I should get Aedan."

He shook his head. "We don't need Aedan. It's time to meet your opponent."

My stomach turned over. "I've already met her."

He grinned. "Change of plan." He pushed open the door and brandished his cane. "Get in."

I looked around. There was no one else on the street. If I resisted, I'd have to fight with a broken leg.

Heart thumping, I got in the car.

42

AEDAN

I wasn't good at this shit.

"I really—" I sighed and broke off. "I really like her. When I'm with her, I feel—"

I broke off again and shook my head. Maybe this had been a bad idea. I'd been hitting the bag at the gym, not long after Sylvie left, when it'd suddenly hit me that he and I needed to have this conversation. And once I thought of it, I couldn't get it out of my head.

"Sylvie is...she really cares about other people. Even me. Christ knows why. And she makes me feel—she *makes me* a better person." *Jesus, that sounded stupid.* I kicked the bed, which made more noise than I'd expected. "Shit. Sorry."

Alec didn't respond.

I stared at his motionless body. "Why am I talking to you? You can't even hear this."

I sat there in silence for a few seconds, listening to the hiss and bleep of the machines. *This is stupid!* But at the same time, it felt right. And God knows, it was about time I did something right.

"What I wanted to say was...I want to be with her. All the time.

Like, long-term, into the future. I haven't told her that part yet. I'm crazy about her. I'll take care of her. I promise."

Alec lay there impassively. But I still felt better.

I stood up. "I gotta go," I told him. "Sylvie's going to cook." I checked my watch and realized I'd better hurry. She'd be home by now, waiting for me.

43

SYLVIE

With every mile we traveled, my confidence drained. What the hell was going on? What *change of plan?* Had he found some other woman for me to fight—someone I couldn't beat? But Rick remained tight-lipped the whole journey, only telling me to wait and see. By the time we arrived, I wanted to be sick.

This time, The Pit was deserted. I didn't get it, at first. The whole point of me meeting Jacki had been so that the crowd could see us together and get fired up about the forthcoming fight. If there was no audience to see me and this new woman, what was the point?

As Rick led me out into the pit, he saw me looking up at the empty balcony. "I didn't want a whole crowd here," he told me. "I've decided to make your fight invitation-only. We'll move it to a different venue, too. Somewhere more private."

I wanted to run—sprint back up the stairs and out onto the street and not stop until I saw a cop car. But, even if I got away from Rick and his guards, Alec was alone and vulnerable in the hospital. They'd take it out on him. "Why?" I asked, my voice shaking. "Why more private?"

Rick planted the end of his cane on the floor and leaned on it, glancing around at his guards. "I had a think about your little catfight with Jacki. The crowd really liked it when she ripped your top. So I thought: how do we maximize that? How do we turn that up all the way?"

He nodded over my shoulder and I turned.

It seemed to happen in slow motion. My opponent walked out from one of the side rooms. Taller than me. Wider than me.

And male.

44

SYLVIE

He was nearly as big as Aedan. I took in his wide, muscular shoulders and the heavy chest that pushed out the front of his gray tank top. He was at least twice my weight. Under his ripped jeans, his thighs seemed as big around as my waist. A bear of a man. His hair seemed unnaturally light blond, as if he'd dyed it, and his eyes were a cold, cold blue. A good-looking guy, but there was something deeply unsettling about the way he was looking at me. He was the sort of guy who sets your alarm bells ringing, when you see him in a bar. The sort where you're suddenly glad you haven't had one more drink, because then you might go home with him...and you sense something awful would happen.

"Meet Lowell," said Rick in my ear. "He just got out of jail a few weeks ago. He was in for assault...and something else."

Lowell smiled a smile that held no warmth at all.

"...see if you can guess what that was." said Rick.

I felt the vomit rise in my throat. No. Jesus, no. He couldn't mean—

"Go ahead," said Rick, stepping away. "I'll tell you when to stop."

Lowell started towards me. He didn't even bother to raise his fists.

I backed away, looking around me for an escape route. Rick and one guard blocked one of the exits while the other guard blocked the other. There was nowhere to run.

"I can't—I can't fight a guy!" I yelled desperately.

"No," said Rick in a conversational tone. "No, I don't suppose you can."

Lowell was almost on me, now. I swung wildly, trying to remember everything Aedan had taught me. *Keep her at a distance. That's where your advantage is.* But it wasn't a *her*, it was a *him*, and that changed everything. His fists were massive and scarred from years of fighting. One good hit from one of those and I knew I'd go down. And once he had me on the floor—Jesus, Rick couldn't really mean for him to...*did he?*

His fist caught me on the arm and it went instantly numb. I was completely on the defensive, backing away and letting him push me around the whole circumference of the pit. All of the intimidation I'd learned had evaporated as soon as Lowell had stepped into the pit. That primal fear a man instills in a woman had swept it away. *This isn't fair.*

Of course it wasn't fair. *Fair* wasn't the way Rick did things. This wasn't going to even be a fight, not really. It was just a prelude to the main event, when he'd get me down on the floor and—

I heard a clicking sound. Rick was taking photos on his phone—to send to the people he'd invite, I realized. The *really* rich ones, the ones who'd pay thousands just to see a man fight a woman. Fight her and—

Lowell hunkered low and came at me with his arms widespread, growling like an animal. I got in a couple of good hits to the face, but he barely seemed to notice. He just stormed on towards me and I couldn't back up fast enough and—

I went down heavily on my back, Lowell on top of me. His legs immediately pinned mine to the concrete so that I couldn't kick him. His hands grabbed mine and slammed them to the floor, the concrete scraping my knuckles. I cried out in pain.

Lowell bent his head so that he could whisper in my ear. "I

haven't had a really good fuck since I've been out. I'm going to wait another couple of days so I can bang the hell out of you."

I heard Rick's phone going *click click click*. Lowell's chest was mashing against my breasts, the heat of him horribly intimate against my flesh. I wanted to be sick. He leaned down and tried to kiss me, but I kept my lips tight closed and strained my head to the side. Jesus, he was so heavy! I writhed, but I couldn't move even an inch. Tears welled up in my eyes, horror at what was about to happen and frustration at my own weakness.

His tongue toyed with the line between my lips, pushing against it. Forcing them apart.

"Enough," said Rick.

Lowell ignored him. He used his elbow to grind one of my hands into the floor, freeing up a hand to grab at the hem of my top, hauling it up, baring my stomach—

Rick's guards pulled him off me. He stumbled away, grinning and panting and staring right into my eyes.

"Good," said Rick. He looked at me dispassionately. "Try to make it last a little longer on the day, though. It'd be good if you can hold him off for at least a round or two before you...have your fun."

"You can't do this!" I yelled, my voice breaking. "This isn't fighting! It's—someone will call the cops!"

"Not the ones I'm inviting. Some of these guys might act like gentlemen when they're buying companies and drinking at their private clubs, but guys—*all* guys—are just fucking cavemen, really. You heard them cheering, when Jacki tore your top off. You and I both know what they *really* want to see."

I pushed past him and ran for the bathroom. I heard them leave as I bent over the bowl and threw up.

45

AEDAN

I was going crazy when she walked in the door. I'd gotten home a little while before, expecting her to be there, only to find the apartment empty. As soon as I saw her ashen face, I didn't have to ask if something was wrong. I only needed to know what.

She slumped down on the couch. I could see the concrete dust on her face and knew she'd been to The Pit. I could see the lines her tears had cut through it and my insides tightened down into a cold, hard knot.

I took her hands and, between sobs, she told me.

I thought I'd felt anger before. I thought the red rage that descended on me during a fight was anger, or my frustration at how Rick had used me was anger. But I was wrong. You have to have someone in your life you care about more than yourself. Only when someone threatens that person can you really, truly know anger.

I told Sylvie that everything was going to be okay. I made her soup and cuddled her up in some blankets and turned on the TV. And then I called Charlie.

Charlie's job is to process the guys the patrol officers drag in, which means he knows everything that's happening locally and he's got access to the police computers. Exactly what I needed right now...except I'd long since used up all my favors with him.

I met Charlie back when I was fighting, in the days before Rick had corrupted me too much. One of Charlie's cousins was just starting out as a fighter and I gave him some tips. Charlie and I had hung out together but, as I'd become Rick's muscle, the friendship had become more and more strained. He'd told me a thousand times to get out...and then, suddenly, it was too late. I killed Travere and quit fighting. When the rumors went around about a guy dying, most of the cops hadn't known where to start looking...but Charlie did. He came to me, having figured out pretty much the whole thing, and demanded I testify against Rick.

I managed to make a deal with him: he'd keep quiet about what he knew and, in return, I'd talk his cousin out of fighting. His cousin was following in my footsteps, maybe six months away from becoming Rick's next attack dog. I persuaded him to quit the scene and get a legit job instead, and Charlie and I agreed things were square. But the other part of the deal was that I'd stay the hell away from fighting. Something I was only too happy to comply with...until Sylvie came along.

Now, I was going to have to tell Charlie the truth. Except, him being him, I barely needed to. He'd known something was up as soon as he'd seen me in the diner.

"You're in deep with Rick again, aren't you?" he said as soon as he heard my voice.

I looked through to the living room, where Sylvie was staring at the TV. I could tell she wasn't really seeing it. "Charlie, I need to find someone."

"We had a deal, big guy. You said you'd stay away from that piece of shit. Or find some way to bring him down."

Fat chance of that. Rick was too smart to be caught red-handed and we both knew it. But I'd sworn, after Travere, that I'd try. "I swear, if there's ever a way, you can put the cuffs on him personally. But right now, I need your help."

"Have you got any idea how much trouble I could get in, giving you information? *Especially* if whoever the fuck you're looking for winds up dead?"

"This isn't about me. It's about Sylvie. There's a big guy, name of Lowell. Just got out a few weeks ago. Assault and...rape." My voice shredded on the last word.

Immediately, Charlie's tone changed. "He did something to Sylvie?"

"He's going to."

I heard a flurry of keystrokes. "Got him." Charlie paused. "Aedan, let me get him picked up. Got my buddy Ryan out there in a car tonight and it's not far from his beat. He'd *enjoy* taking down a scumbag like this, especially if he resists."

That was tempting, but Rick and his sleazy lawyer might get Lowell off the hook. Besides, I wasn't in the mood for justice. I was in the mood for good old-fashioned revenge. "I'll owe you one, Charlie. Please, just give me an address."

46

AEDAN

Lowell was staying in a motel while he was on parole—the sort with chicken wire over the windows. I figured that the place probably saw enough trouble that someone might actually be watching the security cameras in the parking lot.

So, when he pulled up, I forced myself to wait. Charlie had given me his license plate so I knew I had the right guy. I tailed him to the door of his motel room, palms itching with the need to hit him. I waited until he'd opened the lock...and then I shoulder-charged him into the room.

I kicked the door shut and then it was just us, alone, with no one to interfere. No one to save him. I stripped off my jacket. I didn't want to get blood on it.

He was studying me carefully. A fighter can recognize another fighter. Meanwhile, I was getting the measure of him. Smaller than me, but not by much. A good amount of muscle, but probably faster than me. A dangerous combination.

I didn't give a shit.

He figured it out pretty quickly. "You're with the girl," he said. "The one who's training her. You fucking her? What's she like? Nice and tight?"

I knew he was trying to goad me into making a mistake and I didn't care. I ran at him, raining punches at his midsection. He grabbed hold of me, swinging me around and into a table. A lamp smashed on the floor and we were plunged into darkness.

I staggered, off balance. He'd been living here for weeks—he knew the room a lot better than I did. Before I could find him again in the shadows, he was on me, kicking my feet out from under me. I went down hard against the table and it crumpled under me like matchwood. His fist caught me across the face once, twice. I tasted blood.

"She's a hot little piece," he grunted. "All that time inside, I was thinking about girls just like her." He jumped up and, before I could get to my feet, his foot lashed out and caught me in the jaw. Pain exploded in my head, white-hot and all-consuming. The room span.

"Don't worry," he told me. "I'm not gonna hit her too hard. I don't want her passed out while I'm bangin' her. I want her to be able to moan my name."

I came up off the floor and slammed into him like a force of nature, bearing him down to the floor. I heard his arm break as he landed, by which point I was pounding on his face. He hit me a couple of times in the ribs, but it barely even registered. Three good punches and he dropped his arms. Four, and he went limp.

I sat there, straddling his chest. He was looking up at me through swollen eyelids, not giving in but not taunting, either. Wondering if I was going to finish the job and kill him.

I wanted to. For the first time in my life, I really wanted to. And for the first time, I really understood the difference between someone like me and a real killer.

She wouldn't want me to. I knew that.

I stood up. Lowell turned his head and spat out a tooth. He clutched at his broken arm. "You're fucked," he managed to croak. "Both of you. You've brought down hell on yourselves. Have you any idea what Rick's going to do now?"

I turned and walked away, leaving him in a pool of blood. I felt sated. And I'd done what I'd gone there to do—there was no way Lowell could hurt Sylvie now.

But, as the adrenaline faded, I knew the scumbag was right: Rick would retaliate. I hadn't had a choice, but I'd just made things worse.

Minutes later, I found out how much worse.

47

AEDAN

I didn't even make it home. Rick's goons picked me up on the street, halfway back to my apartment, and bundled me into a car. I knew it was pointless to resist. Better that Rick took it out on me than on Sylvie.

Back when I'd been fighting for him, Rick had operated out of a fancy apartment downtown. These days, he'd moved up in the world. The goons pushed me up the gangplank of a gleaming white yacht in the harbor. Inside, it was all antique-effect wood paneling and polished marble—expensive, but gaudy.

Rick was sitting on the edge of an ornate desk, waiting for me, tapping his cane against his leg. His goons let me go and took up positions by the doors.

"Aedan." he said, spitting my name out, and immediately I knew it was bad. He didn't move—he barely even looked at me. But his cane went *tap tap tap* even faster.

Well, fine. I was plenty mad myself. "You bastard. What were you thinking? Even back when I knew you, you wouldn't have done *this*."

Rick gave me a toothy grin. "I hung out with the right people. People who have enough money that they don't have to worry about right and wrong. They just want to be entertained. And I had Sylvie all set up to wow them. Ten thousand dollars *each,* I was going to charge. I had over eighty of them on the guest list. You do the fucking math."

He lazily unscrewed the fat crystal at the top of his cane. When it came loose, he lifted it off. On the underside, hidden inside the cane, was a long, test-tube-shaped vial of white powder. I'd seen coke vials before, but they'd been tiny, enough for a few lines. This was the size of a fat man's finger. Of course— with Rick, everything had to be bigger and better. I watched as he tapped out a long line on the desktop and then bent to snort it. Jesus, he must be putting a thousand dollars a day up his nose.

I glanced around at the yacht, feeling sick. I'd known that he'd gotten worse, since I knew him, but I'd underestimated how much worse. The money had made him hungry for more money and now he was in a downward spiral. He'd do anything if it kept the rich going to his fights. "Lowell isn't going to be hurting anyone," I told him. "I broke his arm."

Rick stood up, his eyes wide, his pupils huge. "You think that changes anything? You think I can't find another guy like Lowell, *tonight?*" He walked towards me. "Jesus, Aedan, think about what I'm offering: the guy gets to beat up a woman and then fuck her, with a guarantee that she won't go to the police. *He* should be paying *me.*"

I gauged the distance between us, trying to estimate whether I could break his neck before his goons got to me. He was just a few feet too far away, and he knew it. And he was right: beating up Lowell hadn't done anything. Except to make him mad.

"You need to learn a fucking lesson," spat Rick. "You don't want to see her get fucked? Fine. You can see her die, instead. You know the only thing better than sex and violence? A Roman fucking circus. A fight to the death. People'll sure as hell pay to see *that.*"

I stared at him. "You won't find a fighter to do it. Not *to the death.*" A body meant far too much heat, even for some of the scumbags in the underground circuit.

Rick just grinned at me. And the true horror of it slowly dawned.

"No," I said quickly.

"You and Sylvie walk into the pit," he said. "And only one of you comes out."

I shook my head.

"Refuse to fight," said Rick, "and I kill both of you."

"No! Jesus!"

"Run, and I hunt you down and kill both of you *and* her brother."

I stared at him, breathless. My heart felt like it was trying to break through my ribcage. I was terrified. I was raging. I know I couldn't do a damn thing about it. "You can't do this!" I yelled.

He just smirked at me. He knew he had me in the perfect trap. Al and Carl were there to stop me killing him, so that wasn't a way out. If I refused to do it, he'd just kill Sylvie himself.

"I can't do it," I croaked. "I can't kill her."

"I didn't think so," said Rick, leaning forward on his cane. "So you'll just have to convince her to kill you."

48

SYLVIE

"I'm slow," Aedan told me. "Use that! Come on!"

We'd been in the ring all morning. He was driving me hard and yet, at the same time, he was giving me lots more openings than usual. It was almost as if he wanted me to hit him.

I shook my head. "But how do you know *he'll* be slow? The guy replacing Lowell?"

Aedan had returned, the night before, and told me that Lowell wouldn't be fighting me. The blood on his knuckles told me why. But he'd also said he'd seen Rick, and that I'd be fighting someone else.

"I just know," said Aedan. "He'll be big, but slow." I'd never heard his voice so strained. "You've got to go in fast and go for the head. Don't let his size faze you. Don't be intimidated. No matter what."

"You don't understand," I told him. "It's not a normal fight. Whoever Rick's got to replace Lowell—he won't just want to win. He'll want to get me down on the floor and—"

"No," said Aedan sharply. "He won't. Not this guy."

"How do you know? How can you be so sure?"

"I just do! Now hit me!"

I stared at him and saw the helpless fear in his eyes. I slowly lowered my fists as realization dawned.

"Come on!" he snapped at me. "Keep going!"

"Oh my God," I whispered. "It's you. Rick wants me to fight you!"

Aedan closed his eyes and lowered his hands. He nodded reluctantly.

"But that makes no sense! He knows we won't fight each other!"

Aedan looked at me from under those heavy Irish brows. "He's not going to give us a choice." He sighed. "If we don't fight, he kills us both; if we don't show, he kills Alec."

I swallowed, thinking desperately. "Okay, so...I have to knock you out? Or you have to knock *me* out?" The thought of doing it made me nauseous, but it was something we could survive.

Aedan shook his head. He put his hands on my shoulders and leaned forward until his forehead touched mine.

"Oh God," I whispered. "Oh, Jesus, no...." I pushed back from him. "*That* was your plan? To train me to fight you and then just show up at the fight and expect me to kill you?!"

He sighed. "I don't know. I figured the later you knew, the better."

Before I knew what I was doing, I'd slapped him hard across the face. "*Asshole!* Stupid, selfish *asshole!* What's the matter with you? I can't do this! You know I can't do this! I love you!"

He stood there, a red mark rising on his cheek, and stared at me. His quiet calm was scarier than any amount of anger. "You have to," he told me. "This is the only move we have left."

"You're *insane!* What are you thinking?! We have to go to the cops!"

"We've got no evidence. If we go to the cops, Rick's lawyer will get him out within hours. And then we're both dead and Alec too. We can't run and leave Alec in the hospital. We don't have a choice. Only one of us can come out of the pit."

"I *can't!* Jesus, of course I can't! Are you kidding me?!" I turned and ran, slipping under the ring's ropes and racing out of the doors of the gym.

He caught up with me half a block away, in an abandoned lot. Seizing my hand, he jerked me around to face him. "You have to." He squatted down so that he was on my level and ran his fingers through my hair. "Sylvie...one of us has to go. And there's no way I'm letting it be you."

I could feel tears pouring down my cheeks, but the deep, hot horror of it was so painful in my chest that they barely even registered. It was too cruel, too twisted. After everything we'd been through together. After finally finding the person I was meant to be with. "*I can't do it!*" I screeched.

He hugged me close. "You have to."

And, underneath the sadness in his eyes, I could see the calm. Jesus, he though—*he thought this was a way to redeem himself!* He thought that, if he sacrificed himself—

I tore myself out of his arms and ran.

This time, he didn't chase me. I ran three or four blocks and only stopped when I reached the docks. It was another beautiful afternoon, with the cranes reflected in glass-calm water. *This isn't right.* It felt like the wind should be howling and the rain lashing down.

I knew Aedan wouldn't kill me. I knew I couldn't kill him. That meant both of us would die at Rick's hands—he'd slaughter us for ruining his big fight. And he'd probably kill Alec in the hospital out of spite.

Some tiny, traitorous part of my brain asked, *isn't one death better than three?*

No. No way. That was giving up everything I believed in. I couldn't conceive of a world without Aedan. The world needed people like him. Any world was better than that—even one without me in it.

The only solution was for me to die. But I knew I'd never persuade Aedan to do it.

So I'd have to do it myself.

49

SYLVIE

At the hospital, I sat at the end of Alec's bed and just watched him breathing. The whole month that he'd been in the coma, he'd been gradually losing muscle tone, his body atrophying day by day, too slowly to notice. Now, though, I saw the difference. I think it's because the same blonde doctor, Heather, was there, checking on him, and the whole scene could have been a month before. Except then, I'd been the frail one and he'd been the strong one.

And now I needed to be strong one last time.

"Tell me honestly," I asked Heather. "Do you think he'll wake up?"

Her shoulders slumped. "It's impossible to say," she said. "I can't make promises—"

"*Please.* I'd give a lot for your gut feeling, right now."

She nodded and stared at Alec. "Then...*yes.*"

"Thank you," I whispered, studying my brother's face. I swallowed. "I need your help."

∼

By the time I'd finished with the doctor, it was evening. I went straight to Aedan's apartment. We didn't even speak, when we saw each other. We just wrapped each other up in a hug and rocked there in the doorway for long minutes.

He eventually pushed me back and looked into my eyes. "You know it has to be me," he whispered. "It's the only way that makes sense. You've got a feck of a lot more to offer the world."

I shook my head. "Don't say that." But my voice was weak and despondent.

He touched his forehead to mine. "Fight's in three hours," he said. "It'll take an hour to drive out there."

"I don't want to spend our last hours talking about this," I told him.

So we didn't. He sprawled out length ways on the couch and pulled me so that I was sitting between his legs with my back against his chest. And he played with my hair while we talked about our childhoods and school and friends and everything that had made us who we were. *I know so little about him!* I thought, horrified.

We sat there as the sun went down inside and the apartment grew dark, neither of us wanting to move, not wanting to waste a single second of precious life. *Why didn't we get up earlier? Why didn't we train less and play more? Why did I work so many shifts at the hotel?* I kept learning new things about him, things that made me love him even more. He hated raspberries, but loved raspberry-flavored candy. He and his brothers had rabbits, when they were kids, and Aedan's used to hide inside his schoolbag and try to go to school with him. He once walked four miles in the rain to get to a gig by his favorite band, then stood there at the front and dripped a huge pile of water—*but the speakers were so loud, they blew me dry,* he insisted.

"Aedan?" I asked at last. "What happened to your family? Why are your brothers spread all over the country? Why don't you talk to each other?"

His arms tightened around me. "Some bad shit. Some bad shit happened."

I waited, but he didn't speak again. "You don't want to tell me?"

I felt him shake his head.

"That's okay." I squeezed his arm. "You don't have to."

"It's not that I don't want to. It's just...it's a family thing."

"Not for outsiders?"

"Not my story to tell."

I nodded silently. As far as he knew, he was going to be the one who died. He was planning to take whatever happened to his family with him to the grave. What could be that awful? I gave a tiny, involuntary shudder.

"I wish it had been different, now," he said, almost as if he was speaking to himself. "I wish I'd looked some of them up. Got back in touch. I wish...." His arms tightened around me again and he put his chin on my head. "I wish a lot of things. Most of all, I wish I could just be with you. Forever."

This isn't right. We shouldn't lose this. We were too good together. To be split apart by an accident would be horrific, but to do it deliberately, to know forever that it was our hands that did it, however unwillingly....

Aedan looked at his watch and then squeezed me. "Time to go," he whispered.

50

SYLVIE

Rick wasn't going to risk holding the fight at The Pit, where regulars could show up. He wanted this to be a private event, with only those who he could trust not to blab. So he'd told us to come to a farm way outside the city. We had to drive there, so I borrowed a car from a friend at work. I didn't tell her that it would be Aedan bringing it back, the next day.

I kept quiet about my plan. When Aedan gently but firmly explained to me that it had to be him who died, I nodded silently. He had to believe I was going to do it, right up until the final seconds.

When we arrived, our cheap, aging car looked ridiculous next to all the high-end SUVs with their chrome and blacked-out windows. There must have been close to a hundred of them, along with a variety of sports cars. No limos, though—the guests had all driven themselves there. They were making themselves accessories by paying to see the fight, so they wouldn't go to the cops, but a limo driver couldn't be trusted not to rat out their employer.

The venue was a large barn. The crowd was already in there, the buzz of excited chatter audible even outside. As we walked towards it, I could see white light streaming out of every crack in the corrugated iron walls.

The big main doors were closed for privacy. Al, one of Rick's bodyguards, nodded us towards a small side door. I took a deep breath, squeezed Aedan's hand...and we went in.

Inside, hay bales stacked two high formed a rough circle much smaller than The Pit's—only about twenty feet across. Two openings had been left on opposite sides for us to enter through and a single hay bale had even been provided for us to slump down on between rounds. Someone had carefully strewn hay all over the concrete floor inside the ring to give it a rustic feel.

Around the ring, the crowd was three deep. Almost everyone was in suits and many of them were chattering as if they knew each other. A few were even talking stocks and shares. *They're doing deals. They're doing business while they wait to see one of us kill the other one.*

Every single guest was a man. I wondered if the men who'd been so eager to see me get raped had come along to watch one of us die. Was that a different sort of man? I wasn't sure.

Both of us wore what we normally wore to the gym—tank tops and sweatpants. We could have been about to train, if it wasn't for the lack of gloves.

We moved slowly through the crowd, but it was no good trying to be inconspicuous. As soon as one person saw us, a cry went up, radiating through the people like a wave. Some cheered. Some leered at me. Some started discussing—loudly—which of us would win.

I noticed that no money was changing hands. Everyone knew this wasn't going to be a traditional fight, where the best fighter won. They weren't interested in betting. They just wanted to see us agonize and sob and brutalize one another.

Several men leaned in front of us and tried to grope me. Whichever way I dodged, there was another hand there to brush a thigh or grab for a breast. Aedan tried to keep me away from the worst of it, but he couldn't be everywhere at once. When one of the men grabbed my ass, he lost it and swung at the guy. The man staggered back, clutching a bloody nose.

"You're still protecting her?" said Rick's voice. "That's kind of ironic, given the circumstances."

He'd pushed his way through the crowd from the other direction and now stood in the middle of the ring, waiting for us. I heard Aedan give a low growl and made sure I had a firm grip on his hand, ready to hold him back if need be. Carl, Rick's other bodyguard, was standing just behind him, gun drawn—there was no need to conceal them, in here. If Aedan attacked, it would all be over in an instant. And I knew the same gun would be used to slay us if we refused to fight or tried to run.

"Have the two of you worked it out between you?" asked Rick. "Who's going to make the sacrifice? I'm genuinely curious to know."

I've never wanted to kill anyone so much in my entire life. Both of us just stood and stared at him, holding hands for strength.

Rick stepped closer to me. "And just think—all this could have been avoided." He reached out and brushed my cheek with his thumb, which made my skin crawl. "All you had to do was *not* tell your boyfriend what happened with Lowell. Then tonight would have been a few minutes of unpleasantness on your back—or maybe on your face—and you both could have gone on with your lives. Although..."—he glanced at Aedan—"he probably wouldn't have wanted you, afterward."

I gripped Aedan's hand even harder, but it was to hold myself back as much as him. I knew Rick was trying to provoke me, to show off to the crowd, and I wasn't going to give him the satisfaction.

Rick rolled his eyes and turned his back on us, quite unafraid. Carl and his gun gave him all the bravery he needed. *"TONIGHT!"* he bellowed, holding his cane aloft for silence, "Two star-crossed lovers face the ultimate decision. How much will they sacrifice for each other?"

The crowd roared. I saw Al close the side door, sealing us all in the barn. He strolled over to Rick, his gun drawn, and took up a position beside him, ready to shoot if we disobeyed.

Aedan pulled me close. Both of us were breathing hard, now, trying not to panic. "You know what you have to do," he told me. "It's the only way. You have to do it."

I shook my head. "I can't!" I knew it was going to be me who lost the fight, but I had to convince him I was going along with his plan.

He knitted his fingers with mine, raising his voice over the crowd. "You can. You can do this. This is the only way we win." And, before I could argue, he leaned in and kissed me, one last time. His lips came down on mine and it was as if he was trying to inject every ounce of his soul into mine, so that he could live on in me.

51

AEDAN

I was ready to die.

I'd made my peace with it, during the walk back to my apartment after seeing Rick, and during the day training Sylvie. I was surprised by how easily I accepted it. In some ways, I guess I'd accepted I might die the very first time I went to fight at The Pit. And God knows the world wouldn't be losing much. I was a pretty good fighter and a pretty average dock worker. The universe would do just fine without me.

What ate at me was the effect it would have on Sylvie. Would she ever forgive herself? I had to make it as quick as possible—in the first round, if possible. I couldn't show pain. If she saw she was hurting me, she'd stop. I had to act like I was fine until I went down and then—

And then what? Would she really keep beating on me, until I was dead? On her own, no. But when she stopped, I knew Rick would be there to scream at her, to tell her she had no choice. He'd threaten Alec. I had to pray that that would be enough for her to finish the job.

Rick had swapped the air horn they used at The Pit for an old brass bell. It sounded to start the fight, the peals echoing off the metal walls, but I didn't want to stop kissing Sylvie. Her lips felt so good against mine. I knew it was the last time I'd ever feel them.

I broke the kiss, took a long, shuddering breath and stepped back, opening my eyes. I lifted my hands and we tapped our fists together for luck. I could see the tears welling up in her eyes and felt the heat of all the anger and pain building up behind my own.

And the fight began.

52

SYLVIE

We stood there staring at each other, fists raised but neither of us moving to hit the other one. Aedan nodded at me. *He wants me to hit him. He wants me to hit him while he just stands there!*

"Fight me!" I yelled over the crowd. "I can't do it if you don't fight me!"

He just stood there, solid as a rock, only his eyes betraying his emotions. I could see every muscle in his arms standing out, every vein.

"*Hit me!*" I screamed.

Rick re-entered the ring, a gun in his hand, and tapped his cane meaningfully on the floor. If one of us didn't make a move, he was going to kill us both.

Letting out a low moan, I stepped forward and swung at the man I loved.

Standing perfectly still while someone hits you is one of the hardest things in the world. Aedan didn't even flinch. My fist glanced off his jaw, a clumsy hit but enough to snap his head to the side. My guts knotted up. *Jesus, what am I doing?*

Aedan nodded at me to do it again.

I couldn't hear anything and I realized the crowd were roaring, the shouts and cheers and leering comments about my body all blending into one noise. Rick was still standing beside us, gun raised.

"I love you," mouthed Aedan. "Hit me."

I hit him, this time putting my full force behind it. I just wanted to get Rick to back off. Normally, my fist wouldn't have even got close to him or, if it did, it would have been like hitting a brick wall. But Aedan hadn't tensed up. He'd left that ripped stomach relaxed and my punch seemed to go right to the very center of him, doubling him over. The crowd roared so loud that my ears hurt.

Aedan struggled for breath. I'd been winded a few times in training, though never that severely, so I knew the bursting, aching pain and the desperate fight for air. It tore my heart apart to see him like that and my mind screamed at me to do something, to stop the monster who was hurting my man.

But I couldn't. The monster was me.

And now I saw Rick turn towards Aedan. His message was clear: he wanted this to be a real fight.

He wanted Aedan to hit me.

53

AEDAN

I straightened up, groaning at the pain in my stomach. And saw Sylvie begin to circle me, dodging and weaving. At first, I was relieved. She'd started to fight. Hopefully now she could get some good hits in and—

I realized she wasn't punching. She was just dancing around me, making it look good.

Giving me a target.

She wasn't doing it for her own benefit; she was doing it for mine. I saw Rick looming nearby, gun drawn, and got the message: I had to hit her, and she was trying to lure me into it.

I lifted my fists...but I couldn't. Sparring had been hard enough but actually hitting her, bare knuckle? I'd never raised my hands to a woman in my life.

"You have to," mouthed Sylvie over the crowd. I could see tears in her eyes.

Behind her, Rick raised the gun. I knew he wouldn't hesitate to shoot both of us, if we didn't give him what he wanted.

I drew back one fist—and saw Sylvie flinch and brace herself. *Oh, Jesus, no!* I couldn't do it if she did that! Christ, she was terrified. *What am I doing?* Even death would be better than this.

My death. But not if Rick killed Sylvie too.

To save her, I had to hurt her.

I did it fast, before she had too much time to be scared. I swung fast and got her right in the mouth. Her head whipped to the side and she cried out...and the crowd roared even louder. *Jesus, the sick bastards!*

When she looked at me again, her lip was split open and blood was dripping onto her tank top. I'd picked the place where it would look the worst, to appease Rick, but where there'd hopefully be no lasting damage. So I was ready for the blood. What I wasn't ready for was the look on her face—the momentary shock and then the deep betrayal. The look that no man should ever, ever see.

I looked at her in horror. Then I lunged at her and pulled her into a clinch, gasping in her ear so that she'd hear me over the crowd. *"I'm sorry!"*

And then the bell went for the end of the round and Rick's goons were dragging us apart.

54

SYLVIE

I sat down on my hay bale. My mouth was filling up with coppery, salty blood and I knew that I'd vomit if I swallowed it, so I spat it out.

Rick had left the ring. He knew that we got it. He knew that we'd finish it, now. The only question, for him and the crowd, was how it played out. Had we made a pact...and would we honor it?

I stared at Aedan across the ring. Both of us had tears in our eyes. Both of us knew it had to happen.

I nodded at him and he nodded back, looking relieved. He thought I was going to go through with the plan. He thought I was going to kill him.

And he had to go on thinking that. Right up until the very end.

The bell went and the final round began.

55

AEDAN

This time, when we came towards each other, our fists were already raised. This time, neither of us was denying what needed to be done.

I felt this overwhelming sense of...relief. She was going to be okay. Sylvie was going to be alright.

Her first punch slammed into my forehead, hard enough to make me stagger. Good. She was going for the head, not wasting time on the body. The head would make me go down and then she could finish it.

The next punch hit my cheek and I heard something crack. I saw the anguished look on her face and I wanted to tell her that it was okay, but she was already lashing out again. I lifted my hands a little, to make it look good, but I made sure it hit me. This time she got my eye and I rocked backward on my heels, pleasantly surprised at how hard she was hitting. She was getting it over fast. That was good.

I saw her reach down and touch the pocket of her sweatpants and I wondered what she had there. Some good luck charm, maybe, or a photo of her folks. Then she put up her guard and came in close. "Hit me," she said quickly. She didn't even have to lower her voice. There was no way the crowd could hear anything except their own insane yelling. "Just once. Under the chin. Make it look good."

I glanced at Rick. Did we need to? He was still outside the ring and looked content to see her pummel me. But maybe she was right. One quick hit on her and then she'd return to me and knock me out and this whole thing would be over.

Forever.

I drew back my hand, feeling sick. *Just do it. One hit. Get it over with.* "I love you," I said.

"I love you, too."

I swung, aiming for her chin. An uppercut that would knock her back a little but not do any real harm.

And everything went wrong.

Just as I swung, she kicked both her legs out in the air, as if she was deliberately flopping onto her back on a trampoline. My punch, instead of making her stagger, sent her soaring through the air.

She landed hard on her back. And she didn't get up.

The crowd fell silent.

I was on my knees beside her in a second. I didn't know how hard she'd hit her head—the roar of the crowd had covered the sound of the impact. "Sylvie? Jesus, *Sylvie?*"

I checked for a pulse. I couldn't find one. Her eyes stared up at me, fixed and unseeing.

I refused to believe it. "*Sylvie?*"

Then I saw how her beautiful angel's hair was turning sticky with blood under her head. "*Sylvie?!*"

No response.

She was dead.

56

AEDAN

"Well, *holy shit,*" I heard Rick say. "I didn't expect *that.*" I was on my feet and across the ring in a heartbeat. I didn't care about the bodyguards anymore. I didn't care about the guns anymore.

The crowd moved out of the way as they saw me coming and that started a general exodus. There was something about the way Sylvie's body lay there on the floor, crumpled so awkwardly, legs stretched out but one hand to her hip. Suddenly, none of those bastards who'd thought they were so brave and edgy for sampling underground entertainment could bear to see it.

Rick's bodyguards slammed into me just as I reached him. I very nearly managed to drag them along with me, but then Al had his shoulder against my chest and Carl was holding my arms behind my back and all I could do was yell and snarl. I was less than a foot away from Rick and I couldn't touch him.

"I guess you get the winnings," said Rick. He was staring at Sylvie's body, genuinely disquieted. He shoved a bundle of bills into the pocket of my sweatpants. "Congratulations," he said coldly. "That's what you get for murdering your girlfriend. You really are a monster."

I remembered how she'd kicked her legs out from under her, ensuring she'd go down hard. She'd wanted to do it.

She'd fooled me. She hadn't gone along with my plan at all. She'd sacrificed herself for me.

The crowd was dispersing quickly. The bodyguards pushed me to the ground and hustled Rick outside. I no longer had the energy to go after them. All I wanted to do was hold the woman I loved.

I crawled over to her body and cradled her head, the blood sticky on my fingers. I closed her eyes. And then I wept and wept, my tears wetting her cheek as if she was crying, too.

57

AEDAN

W hen I finally looked up, Rick and his goons were standing over me. Everyone else had gone.

"Time to go," said Rick. "We'll take her from here."

Al stepped forward to gather her up. He wasn't as careful as he normally would have been. He probably thought I was beyond fighting back.

He was wrong.

As he put out his hand, I grabbed his wrist and *pulled,* putting all my strength behind it. Al flipped over my head and hit the floor with a crack of breaking bones.

"Don't you *feckin' touch her!"* I screamed.

Rick and Carl took a step back. It had happened so fast they were caught off balance. Long enough for me to snatch Al's gun from his holster. I pointed it right at Rick. Immediately, Carl pointed his own gun at me.

"Whoah," said Rick. "Whoah, whoah, *whoah."*

"Get out," I spat. I needed them gone because, in another few seconds, the urge to put a bullet in both of them was going to become irresistible. And Sylvie wouldn't have wanted that.

"We can't leave him," said Carl. "He's got the body!"

Rick ignored him. "You go to the cops," he told me, "and I'll put a pillow over her brother's face."

"No cops," I snarled. "I just don't want you to touch her. I'll bury her. Me."

Rick stared at me for another few seconds. "Let him," he said at last. "If he gets caught, he can take the heat." He backed away. "I don't ever want to see you again, Aedan."

I kept the gun on them until they reached the door, then waited until I heard their car drive away. Only then did I toss the gun away and cradle Sylvie's body again. "It'll be okay," I said, rocking her gently. "I won't let them touch you."

58

SYLVIE

Three hours earlier

Heather, Alec's doctor, listened as I laid it out for her. The Pit. Aedan. My brother's fight. The fight I'd have to have with Aedan. I explained why we couldn't go to the police and then I explained what I needed from her.

"I can't kill him," I said simply. "And he can't kill me. And that means Rick will kill us both. Our only chance is for me to do it to myself."

I swallowed and looked her right in the eye. I spoke slowly and deliberately.

"I need you to give me something that'll kill me," I said. "Quickly. Within seconds. I don't care if it hurts or not. But I need to be able to inject it, so I can do it just before Aedan knocks me down."

Heather's mouth moved soundlessly. "He'll think he killed you!" she said at last.

"I know. And it'll destroy him. But he'll be alive and so will Alec."

She shook her head. "You're talking about suicide! I can't do that! I can't help you!"

"You're saving two lives. If you *don't* do this, we're all dead."

Heather stood up and walked away. My chest tightened because I thought she was going to call security and then the cops, but she started to pace instead. "No. No way. There's got to be another way."

"There *isn't,* Heather. This is the way things are when you're dealing with people like Rick. There are no ways out. Only ways to minimize the damage."

She walked back around to the chair she'd been sitting on and braced herself on it, staring down at the floor, thinking. I sat down, shut the hell up and let her think.

"What if I gave you something to knock you out?" she said at last.

I shook my head. "They're not stupid. They'll see I'm just unconscious. Then they'll try to make Aedan kill me and he won't be able to do it. Then we're *all* dead—Aedan, Alec, me...."

She went quiet again, hanging her head and letting her long blonde hair hang down to cover her face. I could see her knuckles whitening as she gripped the chair. I really thought she was going to snap and call security. But then she spoke and her voice was drawn from somewhere way down deep, as if each word made her feel physically ill. "I can't give you poison," she began.

I stood up. "It's okay," I said. "I shouldn't have asked you. Bleach will work, right? If I get a needle and shoot it into—"

Her head snapped up. "Sylvie, stop trying to be a fucking hero and *listen!*" Her voice was like the crack of a whip.

I shut up.

She took a long breath. "I could mix you something," she said. "Vecuronium would paralyze you. I could put in something to lower your heart rate and breathing. It wouldn't be perfect. Any half-decent paramedic will be able to tell you're not dead. But your boyfriend, in a panic...it'd fool him." She bit her lip. "There's a very good chance it'd just kill you. And there's no way to tell when you'd wake up."

～

Daylight.

That was the first thing that crept into my awareness. A red, warm light. My eyelids were closed. Why were my eyelids closed?

I tried to open them, but couldn't.

There was sound, but it seemed muffled and distant. I was being carried like a baby. Then a softness under my ass and back. I was lying on a bed. *Ow,* my head hurt like a motherfucker.

The bed shook and the room started to move. A car. I was in a car. Stretched out on the back seat.

I hauled and hauled with all my strength but I couldn't get even one finger to move. So I listened, instead, and the sounds I was hearing gradually changed into words.

"—sorry," I heard. "I don't know what I'm going to do, but I swear, when all this is done, I'm going to get that bastard. I'm going to make him pay."

I felt my body roll back against the seat. The car was climbing up what felt like a winding hill. Where was he taking me? Now that my mind was swimming up out of the blackness of sleep, things started to sink in. We'd done it! The plan had worked. Aedan was alive and so was I and now we could move on!

We slowed and then I felt myself roll awkwardly onto my side as the car jerked to a stop. I tried to turn back onto my back but my body still refused to respond. Some of the cocktail Heather had given me had worn off, but not all of it—I was still paralyzed. I wanted to tell Aedan I was alive. He was hurting so much and there was no need. I could grab and hug him and everything would be okay.

If I could *just...move...something.*

I heard him open his door and get out. And then there was a sound that was familiar and yet unplaceable to my drugged brain. A sort of metal scraping and the patter of something soft falling. Rhythmically, over and over again.

At last, he stopped and I heard the rear car door open. I could see only reddish daylight through my closed lids, but I could feel Aedan looking down at me. "I picked a beautiful spot," he said, his voice thick with emotion. "Looking out over the water."

Oh God. Oh Jesus, no. I wanted to throw up with fear. I wanted to scream. But my drugged body just lay there like a lifeless doll.

He leaned over me and wrapped me up in his arms and I felt myself being carried. There was the sensation of being lowered and then cold dampness was soaking through the back of my tank top and the smell of earth surrounded me.

MOVE! But no matter how hard I strained, my body didn't even twitch.

I heard a rustle of clothing and the scrape of his sneakers as he knelt down. When he spoke, it didn't sound like the Aedan I knew. He was stripped down, his soul bared; he was talking the way he talked when there was no one else to hear.

"The first time I saw you," he said, "I thought you were an angel."

Going by where his voice seemed to come from, he was kneeling right beside my grave...but it still sounded horribly far away. The hole must be deep. I was going to be deep down in the earth, with hundreds of pounds of soil on top of me.

"I thought you couldn't be...because nobody would send someone to save a feckin' waste of space like me. I thought I was long past saving. But you showed me—But then I couldn't—"

He took a breath. Something warm and wet splashed onto my cheek.

"—I couldn't save—*God damn it, Sylvie!* It was meant to be *me!*" More wet drops on my face. When he could speak again, he continued. "I promise I'll take care of Alec. And I'll find a way to get Rick. I'll get that bastard, if it takes me twenty years."

I heard him pick up the spade and stand up. "You were the sweetest girl I ever met," he said. "And I will never, ever forget you."

MOVE! I tried to open my eyes, but they weighed a thousand tons each.

There was a *whump* and something heavy and powdery landed across my legs. A few bits bounced as far as my neck.

MOOOVE! But nothing happened.

And the earth kept falling.

59

AEDAN

I put the spade down and looked out across the water. It really was a beautiful place. She'd be happy here.

Jesus, how the hell am I going to tell Alec?

I looked down at Sylvie's grave. I'd thought that she'd have to do this for me—that's why I put the spade in the back of the car. I never thought I'd be the one doing it for her.

I knew I had to finish. She was almost covered up with the first thin layer. I'd left her face until last. I couldn't bear the thought of throwing soil down onto it, the dark clods breaking across those lips.

I stepped down into the hole instead, putting my feet either side of her body. I'd push the earth with my hands, instead. I'd gently cover her face and then I'd just be shoveling earth onto earth and it would be easier.

Jesus, she looked so perfect. Like she was sleeping.

I leaned down and pressed my lips to hers one last time.

And heard a tiny noise from her throat.

I jumped back, staring down at her. But there was nothing else. My eyes filled up with tears. I'd just squeezed her chest a little and the air had moved.

I put both hands behind the earth that covered her stomach and started to push it onto her face.

And her eyes opened.

60

SYLVIE

I couldn't see, at first. My eyes had been closed too long. There was just blinding brightness and then I felt myself being lifted up. Was this heaven?

The shapes resolved and I focused on Aedan's face as he lifted me out of the grave and hugged me to him. He was saying my name over and over again but my tongue was thick and slow and I couldn't seem to move enough air to form words. He put his ear to my chest and listened intently and I knew that it was going to be okay.

He put me in the back seat and drove us a little way away, in case anyone came along and saw the hole and started asking questions. Then he sat in the back seat with me and held me as the drugs slowly wore off. It was another half hour before I could speak again. Full movement took an hour and I was still weak and shaky.

But I was alive. And the very first thing I could do, as soon as I was able, was to pull my man close and never let go of him again.

EPILOGUE

SYLVIE

I called Heather to tell her that the plan had worked. Then I spent a week holed up in Aedan's apartment, going stir-crazy, while we figured out what to do. I'd quit my job before the fight so no one was looking for me, but we couldn't take the chance that word would get back to Rick that I was alive.

Then Heather called to tell us that Alec had shown signs of movement. Apparently, his vitals had started to perk up every time a certain nurse came in and, that morning, he'd opened his eyes.

I picked out the nurse at the nurses' station when we passed, because all her friends were clustered around her saying how great it was. Blonde and curvy. Alec had somehow known, even in his sleep.

When we walked in, he was able to weakly turn his head to look at us.

"Don't exhaust him," Heather told us. "It's going to be a while before he's up and around. But from the tests we've done so far, there should be no lasting damage."

Alec croaked something. I had to put my ear right to his mouth to make out the words. *"Everything feels heavy."*

I hugged him close. "Yeah. I've been there."

Alec turned to look suspiciously at Aedan. *"What's he"*—he coughed—*"doing here?"*

Aedan and I looked at each other. "There's a lot we need to catch you up on," I said. And took Aedan's hand firmly in mine.

Alec stared at our clasped hands...and nodded, still looking suspicious. Then a hint of a smile broke across his face.

"What?" I asked.

"Nothing," Alec croaked. *"Just remembered a dream I had."* And this time, when he looked at Aedan, he smiled.

What the hell is that all about? I turned to Heather. "Thank you. For everything."

"You can thank me by never going near those people again," she said.

I pulled Aedan and Alec into a three-way hug. "Never again."

Alec's recovery took a month, but a lot of it was just rest and physio exercises, so we got him out of the hospital and into Aedan's apartment after just a few weeks. While he healed, Aedan gave notice at the docks and I used the money he'd saved up and the winnings Rick had given him to pay off the hospital bills. Alec and I finally gave up the apartment we'd lived in with our parents. It killed us to do it, but we knew we had to move on. If Rick or someone who knew him ever saw me in the street, we were all in danger.

We talked a lot about where we wanted to go. There was never any question that the three of us would make our fresh start together—Alec and I were inseparable and Aedan and I were together for life. The only thing we had to figure out was where to go. And then, one afternoon when we were sprawled around Aedan's living room fighting the heat with popsicles, Aedan stood up from his chair and said, "Chicago."

AEDAN

"Why?" asked Sylvie.

"It's got the docks—I can pick up some work there, maybe get Alec sorted out with something, too. And options for you—bar work, hotel work...and college, once you get the money together to go back. Good hospitals, if Alec needs them."

"And it's a city, so there'll be a boxing scene...right?" asked Sylvie. "I know you've been thinking about it."

She was right—I had. Ever since Travere had died at my hands, I'd hated the idea of fighting. I'd thought I was the monster, when really it had been Rick. Sylvie had helped me see that and training her had woken something inside me. Boxing was the one thing I did really well. I nodded.

Sylvie folded her arms. "*Proper* boxing," she said. "With rules, and gloves?"

I nodded again. "I want to do it right, this time. I'll have to start at the bottom all over again, but it'll be official. Legit."

Sylvie frowned at me. "There's something else, isn't there? Lots of big cities have ports and colleges. Why Chicago?"

She could read me too well.

"Okay," I said. "The other reason is...the last brother I lost contact with is there. Carrick, the silver-tongued bastard. At least, last I heard, he was there. I don't know how we'll find him, but maybe we could give it a go." I looked her right in the eye. "I reckon maybe it's time." It was exactly what I'd avoided for years. But facing up to death had snapped things into focus. I felt like I had a second chance, now, and I wasn't going to waste it. And if I could find my brother—if I could find *all* my brothers—maybe I'd finally share the horror of what happened to us with Sylvie.

Sylvie grabbed me and pulled me close. "That sounds like a *great* idea. Alec?"

Alec nodded. "Sounds as good a place as anywhere. Fuck it, let's go."

I started scouring the internet for a car that would hold together long enough to get us and our meager possessions to Chicago. But, before we left, there was one last thing we had to set in motion.

SYLVIE

We couldn't be around for it. It had been over a month since the fight, long enough that Rick wouldn't suspect Aedan of being the rat. But all that would be for nothing if Rick saw him hanging around while the police raided The Pit. And if he ever saw *me* again, he'd know he'd been duped.

So we got our road trip underway. We got the call when we were passing through Cleveland. We pulled into a gas station and the three of us leaned against our battered SUV, peering at my phone's screen.

It was a video of the bust, shot by a local news crew. We saw police flashlights light up the gloom of The Pit. The audience turning in horror and trying to run, only to be held back by a small army of police officers.

When they found Rick, he was as smug as usual. He knew there was no hard evidence proving that he'd organized the fights. He could just claim to be another member of the audience. None of the fighters would dare to testify against him.

Except he wasn't going to be arrested for the fights.

Aedan pointed to a police officer. "That's Charlie," he told us.

Charlie pushed to the front and snatched Rick's cane from him.

"You can't do that!" Rick yelled. "That's mine! It's a medical device!"

Charlie grinned. And twisted the crystal top, just as Aedan had told him to. He drew out the plastic vial. "I'm glad you confirmed it's yours," he said. "Because that's a *lot* of cocaine. More than just possession. That's intent to supply, right there."

Rick went pale. I knew what he was thinking—even if his lawyers got the charges to slide, it was enough for the police to get a search warrant for his yacht. God knows how much coke they'd find there, as well as computer records and paper trails that might prove he was the fight organizer. The last view I had of him was his fearful glance at the camera as Charlie slapped the cuffs on him.

No one would ever have to fight at The Pit again.

Aedan shoved the phone back into his pocket. It felt like the end of a chapter. The road, stretching out into the distance, felt like the beginning of a new one.

"I call shotgun," said Alec, slipping into the passenger seat. He was still a little weak in one leg, but he was getting stronger every day. As I watched, Aedan's pet gull flapped lazily down and settled on the roof of the car. It had so far followed us all the way from New York and showed no sign of turning back, as long as we kept tossing crackers out of the window for it to catch.

I stayed outside for a moment, enjoying the sunshine. "Winters in Chicago are meant to be even colder than in New York," I grumbled, pressing myself against Aedan's chest.

"I'll keep you warm," Aedan said, pulling me hard against him. His breath was hot on my neck. "'Long as we get a place where the bedrooms aren't right next to each other. I don't want to be banging you with your brother next door."

I punched him in the arm to shut him up and he tapped me playfully back, and then we were wrestling, giggling and punching and kissing, with a clear road ahead.

The End

Thank you for reading!

Five of my books feature the O'Harra brothers. The order you read the first four in isn't too important because they're all standalones, but you should read *Brothers* last.

Aedan's story you've just read.

The story of Sean, the sledgehammer-wielding badass who teams up with a good girl to save her sister, is told in *Bad For Me*.

The story of Kian, the bodyguard who winds up protecting – and falling for – the President's daughter, is told in *Saving Liberty*.

The story of Carrick, a biker who makes a vow to a woman who saves his life by the side of the road, then returns a decade later to keep his word, is told in *Outlaw's Promise*.

Finally, *Brothers* brings all four O'Harra brothers – and their women – together to search for their missing brother.

Find all my books at helenanewbury.com